NOT
COMIN' HOME
TO YOU

D0095568

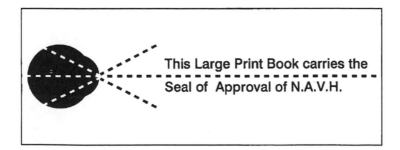

NOT COMIN' HOME TO YOU

LAWRENCE BLOCK

Published in 2005 by arrangement with Baror International, Inc.

Wheeler Large Print Softcover.

Set in 16 pt. Plantin by Liana M. Walker.

Printed in the United States on permanent paper.

Library of Congress Cataloging-in-Publication Data

Block, Lawrence.
    Not comin' home to you / by Lawrence Block.
      p. cm.
    Originally published: Not comin' home to you /
    Paul Kavanagh. New York : Putnam, [1974].
    ISBN 1-59722-058-2 (lg. print : sc : alk. paper)
    1. Serial murderers — Fiction. 2. Large type books.
I. Title.
PS3552.L63N68 2005
813'.54—dc22   2005014153

For my daughters
Amy, Jill, and Alison
and for their mother

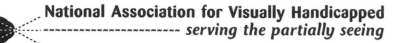

As the Founder/CEO of NAVH, the only national health agency solely devoted to those who, although not totally blind, have an eye disease which could lead to serious visual impairment, I am pleased to recognize Thorndike Press★ as one of the leading publishers in the large print field.

Founded in 1954 in San Francisco to prepare large print textbooks for partially seeing children, NAVH became the pioneer and standard setting agency in the preparation of large type.

Today, those publishers who meet our standards carry the prestigious "Seal of Approval" indicating high quality large print. We are delighted that Thorndike Press is one of the publishers whose titles meet these standards. We are also pleased to recognize the significant contribution Thorndike Press is making in this important and growing field.

Lorraine H. Marchi, L.H.D.
Founder/CEO
NAVH

★ Thorndike Press encompasses the following imprints: Thorndike, Wheeler, Walker and Large Print Press.

"NOT COMIN' HOME TO YOU"

I'm gonna spend this Saturday night
Not sittin' home alone
And I'm gonna spend tomorrow
Not callin' you on the phone
There's hardly time for all the things
I'm never gonna do
And I'm gonna spend the rest of my life
Not comin' home to you

You took my love for granted
While doin' as you please
Now all the seeds you planted
Have grown up into trees
You never saw the forest
Of reasons why we're through
Now I'm gonna spend the rest of my life
Not comin' home to you

You thought I'd always be on hand
Like a book upon a shelf
But you just don't mean half as much
To me as to yourself
And so I walk that narrow line
Not stayin' good and true
And I'm gonna spend the rest of my life
Not comin' home to you

My heart's no good at breakin'
My eyes weren't made to cry
And sorrow's one emotion
I'm never gonna try
So I'm keepin' very busy
Not feelin' sad or blue
And that's how I'll spend
    the rest of my life
Not comin' home to you

From: Phil Posmantur
To: Murray Hutter
Subject: <u>HOME</u> treatment (enc.)

Murray --

I'm sending along the treatment for the last act of <u>HOME</u>. Between the novel and some research I've done on the original case, I think I have a good understanding of the dynamics of the principals.

Assuming it's possible to understand them. . . .

ONE

He stood straight and tall on the ramp of the Interstate, thumb out, waiting. There was a slight smile on his face, and the smile never faded when cars passed him by. He didn't mind waiting. Sooner or later someone always stopped, and you appreciated the lift more when you waited on it.

And damn, he felt good! It was getting on noon and he rocked almost imperceptibly on the balls of his feet, rocked to an inner music and relished the Texas sun on his face and arms. Texas sun or Louisiana sun — he didn't remember crossing the state line, but it might have come and gone while his mind was elsewhere. The trucker who picked him up outside of Meridian was a good old boy who kept the radio full of down-home music and washed it all out with a down-home conversation that was easy to ignore. He could have tuned out the Louisiana-Texas border while tuning out the trucker.

Not that it mattered much. If he was in Louisiana he was on his way to Texas, and if he was in Texas he was on his way out of it. They didn't know him in either state and he wouldn't be around long enough to shake a lot of hands.

His hand moved to his hair, touching it, and his fingers investigated his cheeks and chin. His hair was sand brown, high in front and swept straight back. The sideburns ended a quarter-inch above the bottoms of the earlobes, and his cheeks and chin and neck and upper lip were shaved clean. He had a light beard but still shaved twice a day. He kept his face as smooth as the softest part of any girl he'd ever touched.

It was a habit, this business of touching himself, and he reminded himself again that it was a ritual not to be performed in public. In complete privacy he liked the reassurance of touching all the parts of his body. There was no sexual element in this. Even when he touched his genitals he did so with neither erotic effect nor erotic intent. It was more a matter of continuing self-discovery. All a man had was his own self, and it was as sensible to keep up a dialogue with the body as with the mind. But with the body, as with the mind, this dialogue was a private matter.

Cars passed, and the sun warmed him, and the music sang in his blood and bones. The speed in his veins felt clean and strong and certain. That trucker had been good to him, bought him a breakfast, shook a couple dozen bennies into his palm. He'd lost the breakfast less than fifteen minutes later. He'd half-expected this. It was greasy truck-stop food, and his stomach had known better than to hang onto it. After throwing up he'd gone back inside for a glass of water to clean his mouth, and it seemed at the time that the pills from the night before were wearing off, so he got a second glass of water and washed down two of the bennies. But there was still evidently some of last night's Dexedrine in his system and it went with the bennies in a nice moving way, and his body felt so good and his mind was so strong and he was Jimmie John Hall, free and white and twenty-two, and you couldn't ask for better than that.

Cars in a stream, staring out of blind windshields, going from nowhere to nowhere. Except they all knew where they were going. It was all built into the drivers, stamped beneath the skin of their foreheads like the serial numbers on the engines of their cars, imprinted there to tell them who they had to be and where they had to go and what they had to do.

How small they all were. He had nothing but the clothes on his back and the few things in the airlines bag at his feet and the couple of dollars in his pocket, and he didn't know where he was going and wasn't even sure precisely where he was, and yet he was something and they were nothing, nothing at all.

A car slowed to a stop. He picked up his bag and moved to it, stood while the driver leaned across to crank down the window. A balding, red-faced man, his white shirt deeply sweat-stained under the arms.

"I said how far you goin', boy?"

The car was a Ford, four or five years old, the fenders battered, one of them starting to rust out. The floor in front was littered with cigarette ends and empty coffee containers. The engine, idling now, sounded like a man with phlegm in his throat.

"Hop in, boy. Be goin' clear across to Abilene."

"Thanks," he said. He took a step back. "See, I was just waiting for a friend."

"This some kind of a joke?"

"No. Thanks very much, but I don't want a ride just now."

The man — a salesman, he guessed, with all those cartons in the back seat — was still trying to decide how to react. He couldn't just drive away. He had to make sure nobody was making a fool out of him.

"God damn," he said. "Car ain't good enough for you, is that it? Piece of redneck trash actin' like he's used to Lincolns and Cadillacs. Never heard tell of a hitchhiker puttin' on the style before." He paused, challenging with his eyes, waiting for a response, and he was angered further by the lack of one. His eyes narrowed, turned crafty. "Why, you don't want a ride after all! You're just lookin' to get picked up by some queer. You're a goddamn queer yourself, aren't you, boy?"

He felt his hand moving of its own accord to his back pocket. He stopped the movement and managed a smile. "You got it," he said.

"Huh?"

"I'm a queer," he said. "You're absolutely right." And, still smiling, he turned and walked off a ways in the opposite direction.

He didn't look back. He kept walking, waiting for the car to pull away or for the driver to get out of it and come after him.

15

The piece of pipe in his back pocket rode easy on his hip as he walked, and his mind flashed the image of the pipe leaping into his hand, his shoulder ducking as he spun, the pipe swinging over and down in a neat perfect powerful arc —

Come on. Do something.

Tires spun fiercely. He turned and watched the gravel fly as the Ford pulled back onto the road. He smiled broadly and kept his eyes on the Ford's rear window, knowing the driver was seeing his eyes in his mirror.

No. No, your car ain't good enough for me. It's old and dirty, old man, all the same as you are, and ain't neither of you fit to keep company with Jimmie John Hall.

Damn, he felt good!

He knew the Toronado was going to stop before it had even begun to slow down. It was Wedgwood blue with a white vinyl top, and it was just the sort of car to fit his mood. He wondered sometimes at his ability to anticipate things like the stopping of this particular car. Did he pick up vibrations that gave him a sort of clairvoyance? Or did the force of his own will have something to do with it, communicating itself to

16

the driver and actually inducing him to stop the car? Sometimes a man's will had that sort of power. He was sure of it. If the man was strong enough, and if he knew how to draw himself together and use himself well.

The window lowered at the touch of a button. The driver wore a black mohair suit and a pearl gray shirt with white collar and cuffs. The knot in his tie was small and precise. He had an open weather-burned face. There were a few lines in the corners of his eyes and a tracing of blue veins at the bridge of his nose. He was maybe forty, maybe forty-five.

He said, "Turning off just this side of Big D, if that's any help to you."

"It sure is."

Another button unlocked the door. Jimmie John opened it and swung inside, set his flight bag between his feet on the thick blue carpet, drew the door shut. A buzzer sounded.

"Seat belts," the driver said. "It makes that noise if you don't fasten them."

He fastened his belt and the car moved down the ramp and into the stream of traffic on the Interstate. His face and arms held the heat of the sun, and the stream of air-conditioning on his skin was like a slap of after-shave lotion. The Toronado moved out into the left lane and sat there, cruising smooth and silent at eighty miles an hour.

He said, "This is some car."

"Well, I'll say it suits me. I walked in on that salesman and told him I wanted it with everything on it. Put it all on, I said, figure it all out, and then we'll get down to cases. She's got front-wheel drive, you know. Takes corners like they're straight. Eight-track tape deck, speakers in the rear. What say we have some music?"

"Great."

The driver pressed some buttons and something with a lot of strings came on. The driver asked him how he liked the sound. He said it was terrific.

For a time he tuned everything out. He just sat there wrapped in the cool air and the sweet music and the occasional chatter of the driver, sat there comparing this clean new beautiful car with the old Ford. He had ridden in worse than that Ford and hadn't minded a bit. The truck that picked him up in Mississippi had needed new shocks, and the whole front end was badly sprung, and there was a constant fertilizer smell from the back. But it hadn't bothered him at all because it had suited him at the time.

The whole trick was one of fitting your scene to your mood. Right now he was ready for a little luxury.

After a while he said, "I'm surprised you're willing to pick up hitchhikers in a car like this."

"How's that?"

"Oh, I don't know. Things you read about all the time. Most of the rides I get are in broken-down wrecks. Not anything like this."

The man grinned. "Figure I'm taking a chance?"

"Well, maybe not that exactly."

"Have a look at this. Cuts the chances down some, don't you think?" He opened his jacket to show the fat butt end of a handgun protruding from a shoulder rig. "The hell, you might say I'm still taking a chance. That there is a .357 Magnum on a .38 frame, and it does stack the odds up on my side a bit, but everything you do in this life is a chance, isn't it?"

"I guess so," Jimmie John said. He was thinking about the gun.

"What's life if it's not taking chances? If I never took a chance I'd still be pumping gas for my wife's daddy to this day, taking home eighty dollars a week and waiting on him to die and leave me half the station.

You got to take chances if you figure to amount to anything."

"I guess you're right."

"But what's that got to do with giving somebody a ride? Well, I'll tell you. Like anything else, what it amounts to is a question of taking the *right* chance. Life's full of chances, some good and some bad. Same token, the road's full of hitchhikers. Any time you want to take a chance on a man, whether to give him a job or a ride or I don't care what, you have to know how to size him up. You got to be able to take one quick look at him and learn what it would take a psychologist a couple of years to learn. You see what I mean?"

"I think so."

"Drive along any length of time and you'll see them thumbing rides by the dozens. Guys and girls and you can't tell which is which. Hippie types so many weeks away from a bath you'd be weeks getting the smell out of your car. Now anybody stops for one of them and I have to say he deserves whatever he gets. It's a hell of a thing to say, but I'd have to say it, because a man without the plain sense to take a good look at someone before letting him into his car, he's asking for trouble."

"I guess you're pretty good at sizing people up."

A big smile. Damn, it was easy to tell people what they wanted to hear!

"And I guess you'd be right to say it. Now I look at you and what do I see? Right off I see a boy who cares about his appearance. Shaved, hair combed, pants pressed, clean shirt, shoes shined. Now that's the way to make an impression, and it *ought* to make an impression, because it tells a man right off that here's somebody who cares what he looks like, who gives a damn about the face he shows the world. And then, looking you over a little closer, what do I see? I see a young fellow who's not afraid to smile and look a person directly in the eye and speak up when he's spoken to. Not a kook or a crank, not stoned on drugs, but a decent American boy."

"Well, thank you, sir."

"A college boy heading on back after semester break."

"How did you —"

"Oh, just what I said, a matter of knowing how to take the measure of a man. Anything beyond that is just guessing, but let's just see where it leads us. I'd be inclined to say a Christian school, and would I be far off guessing

TCU in Fort Worth?"

"That's just absolutely amazing."

It had always delighted him that it was so easy to give these people what they wanted. Now the conversation turned to the prospects of the TCU football team, and he found it no problem at all to hold up his end of it. He knew little about football and less about Texas Christian University, had not even known it was located in Fort Worth. But at this point the driver was hardly likely to question his credentials, having taken pains to supply him with them in the first place. *"Now who's that little sophomore scatback you fellows have got coming up?" "Oh, right, I know who you mean —" "Denton, I think his name is." "Right, that's it, Denton."*

The man was apprehensive enough to strap a gun under his arm, but he couldn't recognize a load of shit if you dropped it on his head.

From football the conversation turned to an elaborate discussion of how the driver had come from pumping gas for his father-in-law to driving a crisp new Toronado, and at that point Jimmie John dropped out of it entirely and let it turn into a monologue without an audience, slipping in an appreciative murmur whenever an instant of silence arose to demand it. He caught phrases about the reclamation of wastes in the oil-drilling process, but it hardly seemed worthwhile to concentrate on what was being said. It was so pleasant, surrounded by music and cool air and the white noise of this man's conversation, that he had to force himself to get down to business.

He straightened suddenly in his seat, furrowed his brow in concentration.

"Something?"

"Sounds as though you got a flat."

"Don't hear a thing."

"Maybe it's more feeling it than hearing it, being that I'm on this side. Feels like the right rear."

"Damn if I notice it. Course, softly sprung as this car is, you just don't get that much of the feel of the road surface."

"Do you suppose we better stop? I can change it for you in a minute."

"Service area coming up in four, five miles. They'll do it."

Damn the service area, he thought. He said, "I could change it for you myself, save you a couple of bucks."

"Oh, as soon give them the money as Uncle Sam. Those boys'll make better use of it. Besides, they can get the bolts on tighter. You know, I think that tire just *might* feel a bit soft, now that you called my attention to it."

He waited a moment, then uncoupled his seat belt and turned slightly toward the driver. The buzzer hummed accusingly and a light flashed on and off on the dashboard.

"Something in my pocket," he explained.

"Go ahead. I've got to have somebody disconnect those damned things one of these days. Keep forgetting to get around to it. Not the seat belts. I don't mind a seat belt or anything else that might save my life, but I hate like hell to have an automobile talk back to me."

The length of pipe was snug in his back pocket. He got it out and held it so that his body shielded it from view. He took a few breaths, seeing the whole process first in his mind, picturing all of it. The car was sitting pretty at eighty miles an hour and the nearest other car in sight was way ahead of them, but the driver had a handgun in his armpit, so if he was going to do it at all he had better get it right the first time around.

He moved both hands at once, the left catching hold of the wheel, the right whipping the piece of pipe up and around and down. He hit the driver just over the ear. For an instant the man's hands tightened their grip on the wheel. Then they went slack.

He kicked the driver's foot off the accelerator, replaced it with his own and kept the car steady at speed. The man was limp beside him. He put down the piece of pipe and tilted the rear-view mirror so that he could make out what the hell was going on behind and alongside him. When his opening came he eased his way over to the right-hand lane and slowed down. He pulled off on the ramp to the service area and braked in a remote section of the restaurant lot. The engine shuddered softly and died when he reached across and turned the switch. There wasn't another car within fifty yards of him.

The gun was a revolver, with bullets in five of the six chambers. When he unlocked the glove compartment to put the gun inside he found a box of shells two-thirds full. He didn't bother removing the shoulder holster from the man.

And what about the man, anyway? Put him in the back seat and he'd look to be sleeping, but he could come to without his knowing it, and there he'd be, in back of Jimmie John and with the advantage.

Trunk would be a safe place for him, but the prospect of lugging an unconscious man out of the car and stuffing him into the trunk didn't appeal. All that he needed was one sharp-eyed son of a bitch and it was all up.

He walked around the car, opened the door on the driver's side, shoved the man across to the other side of the car. He got in and drew the door shut and studied the man. The trouble was that he just plain didn't look like a sleeping passenger. He looked like a corpse.

He was alive enough, though. Breathing slowly, but sure as hell breathing. Jimmie John got the seat belt around him and fastened it. After all, the man said he didn't mind a seat belt or anything else that might save his life. Wouldn't want to hit a bump and send him through the windshield.

He turned the key in the ignition and checked the gas gauge. No problem there — half a tank left, so the old boy didn't have to look good close up, just from a distance. He considered for a moment, then hit on the idea of fastening the shoulder belt across his chest. And that did it. When he started the car and pulled back onto the highway, his passenger looked hale and hearty. Taking a nap, maybe, but as healthy as you could reasonably want a man to be.

He drove along, listening to the speed singing in his veins. From time to time he played with various gadgets, repositioning the six-way power seats, cutting off the tape deck and punching in the FM radio, working a switch to make the power antenna go up and down. Oh, it was a fine car, a beautiful car. He felt a special harmony with it. Like himself, the engine had a ton of power in reserve. Even the front-wheel drive seemed indefinably metaphoric of his own approach to life. Instead of the rear end pushing the front along, the front end dug in and ran.

The man beside him stirred once as they came up on the first Dallas exits. A little tap on the head put him back to sleep again.

When he was well clear of the last of the Fort Worth suburbs, he took the first exit and headed north on 281 through Mineral Wells. "You're just not very interesting company," he said aloud to the unconscious man beside him. " 'Fraid it's time we parted company and went our separate ways."

He turned onto a county road and put another ten miles on the odometer, turning onto a smaller road whenever an intersection gave him a choice. The countryside was flat and empty, a few pecan groves but mostly the endless stretch of grazing land. On a two-lane gravel track in the middle of nothing much he pulled over and cut the engine. He unhooked the shoulder belt and made a careful search of the man's pockets.

Walker P. Ferris. That was the name on the license and all the credit cards. Walker P. Ferris of Balch Springs, Texas, wherever the hell that was. Well, old Walker wouldn't have too much walking to do, at least being left in his home state. He'd be up and around within the hour, and even a road like this one would have someone drive down it sooner or later. If the driver turned out to be a judge of character on the order of Walker P. Ferris himself, good at taking the measure of a man in a single glance, then old Walker would have nothing to worry about.

Except —

Except, damn it all, he *liked* this car. He could leave old Walker at the side of the road and figure on eighteen or twenty hours before the balloon went up, which would be plenty of time to drive where he was going, and then he could leave the car somewhere and let them find it and give it back to old Walker P. Ferris.

He got out of the car and looked at it. Even prettier outside than in. A shame to dump it, now or later.

And hadn't old Walker spelled it all out in the first place? A man had to take chances. What was life if it wasn't taking chances? Who the hell wanted to pump gas for eighty bucks a week?

He started the engine and ran the car a couple of hundred yards off the road. It was no jeep, but the pasture wasn't that much rougher than the road had been and he didn't feel any rocks snapping at the underside. He undressed Walker P. Ferris and stowed his clothes in the trunk. No point leaving signposts as to just who old Walker might be.

He dragged Walker out of the car and spread him out on the grass. He took the length of pipe and struck twice, full strength, just above the bridge of the nose. He felt bone give way with the second blow. He listened for breathing, felt for a pulse. Nothing. No evidence that old Walker was living, but damned if he seemed any different now that he was dead. He hit him once more in the same place for insurance and wiped the pipe in the grass before returning it to his hip pocket.

Not that he particularly needed that piece of pipe. He had himself a revolver now, and even a shoulder rig to wear it in, if he wanted to go to the trouble of wearing a jacket over it. Seemed as though it would be easier to stick it down under his belt or something like that, but he had all the time in the world to worry over that.

He took another of the trucker's bennies. Not that he felt the need, but the speed edge was starting to wear the slightest bit thin and he didn't just yet want to let go of it. He was feeling real good and he wanted to ride the crest of that feeling as long as he could.

He drove back to the gravel road, turned back in the direction he'd come from, and with unerring instinct retraced his route to 281. He hadn't even made any particular point of remembering the turns he'd taken, but when you were working at top form you didn't have to; it all stuck in your brain and waited there until you needed it, and then it all came to you. If you knew how to make it work. If you knew how to get inside yourself and on top of yourself and make it all work, make everything work.

He drove north on 281. He bought gas in Wichita Falls and sat back cool and proud while the attendant made a fuss over his car. *His* car — why, it had really been his car from the moment it stopped for him. From the moment he willed it to stop. Even before, for why else had he sent the old Ford packing? All along he'd been waiting for this particular car to come and belong to him, and it had come provided with a gun and a box of shells and a man who was good at sizing men up and taking the right kind of chances.

The car took eighteen gallons of gas but didn't need oil. No, it wouldn't be an oil burner, not this car. Very low maintenance costs. And the lowest possible initial cost.

He crossed the Oklahoma line and stopped at a Burger King in Lawton for a cheeseburger and coffee. After eating he stood around for better than fifteen minutes, waiting to see if the food would have to come back up again. But it stayed down, and finally he knew it was going to stay down permanently, and he got back into the car and drove north.

Well, I would say I knew the boy.

Now this is going a ways back. I was living common-law with his Ma, Ellie Hall, or Ellie Jenks which was her maiden name that she sometimes used. Hall, she must of told me his first name but it's slipped my mind, he was long gone before I came in the picture. I lived with her common-law for a year or thereabouts.

As far as the boy is concerned, I would have to say he was all right. To be truthful I didn't have too much to do with him. He kept to himself mostly. I was working days when I worked, which was pretty steady then, so I wouldn't see him much aside from breakfast and supper. I sometimes gave some thought to being a daddy to him, taking him fishing and such, but it never came to that.

He was a boy kept to himself a good deal. I do recall he was always neat and clean about his person. He was respectful, too. If he gave his mother any grief I honestly don't recall it.

I have this memory of him playing with a slingshot. He would just sit out back of the trailer afternoons with this old slingshot and a pocketful of pebbles and practice with it. There was rats prowling about the garbage and he would go after them with the slingshot. I don't suppose he ever hit anything but he would pass the hours that way.

See, this was ten, twelve years ago, and him just a young boy at the time. I don't know if it was a whole year I lived with her or not. The way I started, I just thought I'd keep company with her for a short time, and it stretched out to longer than that. She was a pleasant woman, easygoing, and didn't make no trouble for a person. She would like to take a drink or two and just talk easy about any old thing. Why I left, my cousin over Waycross got this service station and wanted me to help him run it. So I went.

Never did see Ellie after that. I had word of her a couple of times. Now a couple of years back I do believe somebody told me she was in the hospital. I have a memory that it was the state hospital, something to *do with the mind, but I could be wrong about that. Whether it was, and whether she's still there, I would have no way of knowing, but you could find out about that, I'm sure. Just a question of knowing who to ask.*

About the boy, I would have to say I've had no thought of him in years. I was little to him and he was little to me and I moved on out and forgot about him.

Since all this came up, and realizing it's Ellie's boy, why, I'll sit back and try to recall him to mind. But what I keep coming back to is how little I do remember. Just that he was there. That he was in the background. And such little things as him practicing with the slingshot. To be honest, I can't even get a clear picture of him in my mind. Just that he always stood up straight and tall. I believe he was tall for his age and I remember his posture was good, not slouched over like so many boys tall for their years.

Also his eyes. I remember his eyes, and the way he looked at a person.

TWO

Mr. McCulloch was talking and she just couldn't make herself concentrate on a word he was saying. This was sort of a shame because she liked Mr. McCulloch, she really did. He was awfully young for a teacher. Twenty-five or thereabouts, certainly no more than thirty, and most of the teachers at Grand Island Central had been saying the same dull things since the Spanish-American War. Not in the same building, of course. Six years ago they had finished building the new high school, and the old brick building at the corner of Palmer and Whitemeadow had since been converted into another elementary school. Her sister Judy had been in the last class to graduate in the old building. Judy had not been able to graduate, of course, but that was the class she'd been in.

One of these days Judy would come for her. No, not *come* for her — Judy would never come back to Grand Island, Nebraska, not if they made her the mayor. She remembered that parting scene, Judy on the porch, her father in the doorway, the words flashing like knives. *"Out of here, you whore! Off my property!"* *"You'll never see me again, goddamn you!"* *"Never's too soon for me. This is a decent house."* *"Keep your decent house. Keep your whole fucking town."* *"You don't use that language here, you little —"* *"Don't you touch me! You touch me and I swear I'll kill you!"* *"Just you get out of my sight."*

No, Judy would not come back. She would not set foot in Grand Island, probably not in the whole state of Nebraska. But someday Judy would send for her. There would be a postcard or a letter or a telegram, or the telephone would ring and her mother would answer it and say wonderingly that there was a call for her, a long distance call for her, and it would be Judy. "You pack your things and get on a bus, Betty Marie. It's time you got out of that hole and took a look at the world."

Someday.

And then Judy would take her away, and the two of them would live together in a clean apartment in a brand-new building. Judy would help her get a job as a stewardess, and sometimes they would work the same flights together, the Deinhardt sisters, always bright and cheerful and pretty, always knowing the right thing to say, never too busy to help a mother with a sick baby or ease the fears of a passenger flying for the first time.

She was pretty sure Judy was a stewardess. It was the kind of thing Judy would do. Unless she'd become a nurse. That was also a possibility, and she wasn't quite sure which way she would prefer it. There was more glamour to being a stewardess, all that travel and excitement, and the interesting people you met. But nursing also had a lot to be said for it. She could picture Judy in a starched white uniform, standing at a doctor's side, passing scalpels and sutures in a tense open-heart operation. Or making the rounds in a terminal ward, her heart heavy with sorrow at the inevitable fate of her patients, but the smile on her lips and the music in her voice calming the nerves of those poor doomed men and women. And *she* could do this too. Judy would help her, would guide her, and the Deinhardt sisters would be the bulwark of the hospital's nursing staff, always prepared for any emergency, an inspiration and comfort to doctors and patients alike.

In her notebook she wrote: *Elizabeth Deinhardt, R.N.*

She could never seem to stop writing her name in class. Once Miss Tuthill had demanded to see her notebook, and she'd wanted to die of embarrassment. Page after page of permutations of her name. *Elizabeth Marie Deinhardt. Betty Marie Deinhardt. Betty Deinhardt. Bette-Marie Deinhardt.* And, occasionally, the verbal fulfillment of various fantasies, her name coupled with boys in her classes, boys who scarcely knew she was alive. *Elizabeth Fuhrmann. Mrs. Kenneth Fuhrmann. Mrs. Stephen Carmichael. Betty Marie Carmichael.*

"I don't see how this will help you learn American history, Betty. Do you?"

"No, Miss Tuthill."

"Some students find it helps their concentration when they doodle or draw pictures in their notebooks. But I don't think you could have been concentrating on your classwork when you wrote all this. You were off in some private reverie, weren't you?"

"I guess so, Miss Tuthill."

"You're an intelligent girl, Betty, but I must say it doesn't show in your classwork. I think you'd be well advised to concentrate more on what we're discussing in class and less on what your name may be in years to come.

"I'm sorry, Miss Tuthill."

But she just couldn't. Even when nothing else filled her mind, even when she paid the closest possible attention to what was being said, the words simply refused to stay in her mind. She heard them and forgot them simultaneously. And in this class, Mr. McCulloch's class, it was even worse. She couldn't understand algebra. She just couldn't understand it, period. It didn't make any sense to her. It was just numbers and letters and they went together in some mysterious way and none of it made the slightest bit of sense to her.

She didn't see how she was going to pass algebra. She would probably squeeze by in history and English, and she would get a good mark in Spanish because it just seemed to come to her automatically, but she was sure to fail algebra. Unless Mr. McCulloch just passed everybody out of sheer desperation, to be over and done with them. But even if she passed everything she still had another full year to get through before she could graduate, and she didn't see how on earth she could manage it. Another year of sitting at these little desks and writing her name all over her notebook. Another year of dreaming about boys while none of them asked her out, none of them walked with her, none of them even spoke to her. Another year of eating TV dinners in front of the television set and listening to her parents argue and pretending not to notice when her grandmother passed gas. Granny did it all the time, she didn't seem to notice it herself, and whatever room she was in would reek in no time at all.

And it gave her parents something else to fight about, her father yelling that he was sick of that old woman stinking up his house, her mother replying that it wasn't his house in the first place, that it was Granny's house, and if it wasn't for Granny they wouldn't have a roof over their heads. They had that fight at least twice a week, delivering their lines as if they had them carefully memorized, and through it all the old woman would sit impassive, not taking any notice of what was going on around her, and more often than not cutting loose with a beautiful one right in the middle of it all.

At least Granny never argued with anybody. At least Granny never bossed her, never made her feel like an insect. A little gas wasn't that awful. Everybody did it, after all. It was just that the old woman did it constantly.

Chalk squeaked on the blackboard. Mr. McCulloch was writing something with a lot of X's and Y's in it, and numbers and parentheses and decimal points. She prayed he wouldn't call her to the blackboard to do the problem. She wouldn't have the faintest idea where to start.

Except it wasn't a blackboard. It was green, and you wrote on it with yellow chalk. All of the blackboards in the new high school were green. It was supposed to be easier on your eyes, although she had never noticed any difference herself. You would think they would call them greenboards, but instead they always called them green blackboards. If it was green why call it a blackboard in the first place? It was like saying you were going to take a drink out of a plastic glass — if it was made of plastic, where did you get off calling it a glass?

No one else had ever commented on these things. She thought it was very interesting, words and expressions where an old outgrown meaning was left hanging around like that. She had lots of interesting thoughts, she really did, but nobody knew this about her. Nobody really knew anything at all about her except her name and what she looked like and where she lived and what seats she occupied in various classrooms. No one on earth knew the person she was, except possibly her sister Judy, and Judy had moved out six years ago and had never even sent her a post-card.

Unless her mother got the mail and tore up Judy's cards without showing them to her. Sometimes she liked to believe that, but other times she was pretty sure Judy never wrote those cards in the first place.

What was wrong with her, anyway? She was a few pounds overweight, but Ellen Hacker was at least twenty pounds heavier than she was and that hadn't stopped Raymond Gault from going steady with her for months. She got a couple of pimples once in awhile, but June Woodhead had bad acne all over her chin and that didn't keep boys from taking her to parties and movies. She knew what it was — all those girls had personality, and she didn't.

But she *did.* She had all these thoughts inside her, only nobody knew about them because nothing ever came out. She was an interesting person. She *was.*

Judy was right. A person couldn't stay in a town like this, couldn't live in a house like the one she lived in with a family like hers. A person had to go out into the world.

If only she was like Judy. If only she had the nerve. If *only.*

The bell rang. It always did, sooner or later.

· After her last class she went to her locker for her jacket. Linda Jensen and Patti Stryker were talking in the next aisle. They were discussing the propriety of letting a boy take you to a drive-in. Linda was saying, "What it depends on is the boy. I mean, it's all up to the individual. If you trust him it's one thing, but if he's got a reputation, you know, then you're going to have a reputation. Not mentioning any names, but you know what I mean."

She had only been to drive-ins with her parents. Once in a while her father would be in a good mood and they would do something as a family. It always made her feel good when they started out, but it never stayed good throughout the entire evening. Sooner or later something invariably went wrong and she wound up sorry they went at all.

There were two drive-ins nearby, one just south of town, the other on Route 30 about halfway between Grand Island and Central City. In Grand Island itself there were two regular movie theaters. The Grand now showed nothing but X-rated films. The Orpheum was running a picture with Ali MacGraw and Steve McQueen. She had seen it the day before yesterday and thought about seeing it a second time.

She started walking toward the theater, then changed her mind. The bill was due to change tomorrow, and she had seen the coming attractions and wanted to see the new picture. She couldn't remember the name of it now, but Robert Redford was in it, and Cybill Shepherd, and she liked them both. She couldn't really afford movies two days in a row.

She walked home. There was a bus she could have taken but it was a nice day and she preferred to walk. It wasn't to save money; she wound up stopping at the Corner Lunch and spending more than busfare on a Coke and *Screenplay* magazine. She walked because walking took longer and she wanted to postpone returning to her house.

She spent a long time over the Coke and read most of the magazine, carefully tucking it into her schoolbag before continuing on home. Her father didn't approve of the movie magazines, though whether his objection was based on their moral content or the expense they entailed she couldn't determine. They *were* a waste of money. She had to admit that. The stories never told you as much as the titles promised, and she'd heard on Johnny Carson that most of them were all made up anyway by the writers. Something made her buy them just the same. It was something to do, something to take your mind off things.

It was almost five when she reached her house. The sun was at her back, and the windows of the house threw its rays back in her eyes. Usually she looked at the house without seeing it. Today it seemed to sum up her whole family, her whole miserable life. It needed paint all over, and on the weather side the clapboards were almost completely exposed. There was a gap of several feet in the porch rail where her father had fallen against it almost two years ago. The lawn was more mud than grass; in the spring it would sprout up in weeds, and once or twice during the summer her father would attack them with the mower but the rest of the time they'd grow without interference. You couldn't expect much grass to grow there anyway, not with broken-down cars parked all over the place. Five cars they had, and only one of them ran, and you couldn't depend on it. The others just sat there and rusted.

The cars were her father's main interest. He would spend long summer afternoons working on them, crawling underneath them, tinkering with this and that, sometimes managing to get an engine started, sometimes actually rendering one of them briefly mobile. They would never really run properly. They would never be worth anything. They just occupied time that Frank Deinhardt had no better use for, and helped him work up a thirst.

One of these days. One of these days she would get out, out, out. Judy would call — she *had* to. Or, if that never happened, then she would get out on her own. To a place where boys would like her, and girls would be her friends, and she would be alive and real. There was sure to be a place like that somewhere in the world. The whole world was not Grand Island, Nebraska.

Her mother said, "Well, look who's here. Where were you so long?"

"At Carolyn's house. We were studying."

"Carolyn's house. You certainly spend a lot of time over there."

"It helps when you study with someone. The teachers recommend it."

"Do they now. I wonder why it is that you're always over at Carolyn's and she's never over here."

"It would be out of her way. She lives right on my way home from school, but it would be out of her way to come here and then go home."

"I don't suppose it's that you're ashamed of where you live. You and your sister both, too good for the people you came from. What's this Carolyn's last name? You told me but I forget."

"Fischer. Carolyn Fischer."

"And she lives where?"

"Newgate Avenue. Near the viaduct."

"I don't know any Fischer."

"They just moved here a year and a half ago. Her father works for the B & C."

"Does he now." Florence Deinhardt seemed to be gathering herself for another attack. Then she gave it up and her shoulders dropped. She looked old now, and defeated. Betty looked at her mother's face and saw nothing but disappointment.

Now she was saying, "Well, you missed supper. We ate early on account of your father having to see a man. Or saying he had to see a man, don't ask me which. There's some cold meatloaf if you want to fix something for yourself."

"I had a sandwich over at Carolyn's."

"You know better than to eat in the afternoon. Spoils your appetite for supper."

But there *is* no supper, she thought.

She walked on into the living room. Her grandmother was in her rocker in front of the television set. She was watching a toothpaste commercial. The boy and girl in the commercial had greenish faces.

She said, "Hello, Granny."

The old woman looked her way and smiled, her eyes not quite focusing on Betty's face. She had her teeth out again, Betty noticed. She had a perfectly good set of teeth but simply would not wear them. It was more disgusting than the farting. That was something she couldn't help, but she could certainly take the trouble to put her teeth in in the morning.

She went upstairs to her room, read a couple of stories in the movie magazine, then put it away. According to Ann-Margret, you didn't have to pet to be popular, and the most important thing was to be a good listener.

There was a Spanish test scheduled for the morning. She spent awhile studying for it and listening to her radio. She didn't bother with the algebra homework. She didn't understand any of it and it made her head ache to think about it.

She turned off her light and her radio when she heard her father's car in the driveway. She got undressed and under the covers and pretended to be asleep.

She lay awake for what seemed like a long time. She was hungry, and the cold meatloaf, unappealing when her mother had mentioned it, now struck her as the ultimate taste sensation. Cold meatloaf and ketchup and bread and butter and a glass of milk —

But it wasn't worth getting out of bed. And it wouldn't hurt her to miss a meal. Maybe if she took off a few pounds, and if she saved up some money and sent away for the Mark Eden Bust Developer, which she was sure they couldn't advertise all over the place if it didn't do *some* good —

Maybe if she did those things and others, maybe someday someone would notice her. Someone. Someday.

Maybe.

I cannot say I knew Elizabeth very well. It's unfortunately true that one has very little contact with a large number of one's students. I get to know the very good students and the very bad students, the discipline problems. Elizabeth was an average student, perhaps slightly below average, and certainly not a discipline problem.

You hardly knew she was there. In a sense I don't suppose she was. She was not responsive. I don't suppose she learned very much American history in my class. She attended classes, she did her homework, and that was all.

I always thought she was nice. I sat behind her in one class and she seemed like a nice kid. Sometimes I would borrow a pencil from her or something like that.

She was just, you know, one of the kids I knew in class. I never had a real conver-

sation with her or anything.

When all this happened I just couldn't believe it. I mean, she wasn't the kind of person something like this would happen to.

It really makes you think.

I found her an excellent language student, responsive and interested. She was quiet in class but turned in her assignments faithfully and had an intuitive feel for Spanish.

I feel certain there's more to this than we understand at the present time.

THREE

He stayed with Route 281. At Fort Sill, a
few miles north of Lawton, most of the
traffic swung northeast on the Bailey Turn-
pike. He almost turned with them but
changed his mind at the last minute. It was
a better idea to avoid toll roads and major
highways, at least for the next couple of
hundred miles.

Just past a town called Geary he drank a
cold Coke while a kid with copper skin and
straight black hair filled the gas tank. The
kid wasn't as awed by the car as the one
who had filled the tank earlier. When he
went to put the Coke bottle back in the
rack he noticed a few other boys and men,
all with the same color skin and the same
straight black hair, and he realized that
they were all Indians. That explained it, he
decided. Either Indians weren't that impressed by cars or they weren't the sort to
let their emotions show. He thought it over

and decided he preferred the second explanation. He liked the idea of Indians all over the whole damn country just sitting around on their blankets and being real cool about things.

He had paid cash for the first tank of gas. And that, he'd since decided, had been a mistake. Old Walker P. Ferris might have had half the money in Texas, but you wouldn't know it from the amount he'd been carrying. Eighty-three dollars and a handful of quarters and dimes, and that wasn't enough to fill the Toronado's big old tank too many times.

Credit cards, though, would keep it full forever.

Of course the cards took a little thinking about. Sooner or later they'd turn up Ferris, whatever the buzzards left of him, and figure out who he was. And sooner or later it would occur to some brilliant peace officer to wonder where old Walker's car had gone to after Walker had quit traveling in it. A batch of credit card slips scattered over a batch of states would point that out pretty accurately.

But that would take its own sweet time to happen. The boys who sold him gas would just pop those slips in the box without a second look, and then they would send them on to the card companies, and it wouldn't be until the bills went out to Walker P. Ferris himself that anything would show up. And that would be weeks or months, and by that time he'd surely be shut of the car and off in a different direction altogether, so what was the point of worrying about it?

He hadn't even bothered practicing the signature. He just studied it for a time, and while he drove he played at picturing the signature in his mind, picturing too the way his hand would move to write the name just as Ferris had written it. And that was better than practice. It was actually doing the thing when you could make it happen that way in your mind ahead of time. Same as the move he had made on Walker, ducking and pivoting and grabbing for the wheel and hitting Walker upside the head all at once, and it came so easy because it had all been rehearsed, not just the what of it, the act, but the whole feeling and internal sensation of it.

He sauntered over to the car while the Indian kid finished wiping the windshield. He gave him the plastic card and leaned up against the front fender, waiting. When the kid went into the office he experienced a sudden unexpected rush of nervousness, but he guessed almost at once what it was all about. The boy was out of sight, that was all, and people became more of a threat when you couldn't keep an eye on them.

He was never afraid of anything he could meet eye-to-eye.

And when the boy came back and presented him with a little plastic tray with a slip clipped to it, he signed next to the *X* without a bit of hesitation. And wrote *Walker P. Ferris* as well as Ferris himself had ever done. And gave back the pen and accepted the card and the receipt and drove off.

The tapes were all the same, strings and muted woodwinds, music to suck eggs by. He played the radio as he drove but kept switching stations because he couldn't find the kind of music he wanted to hear. He picked up a wide variety of stations, country music and rock and classical, but whatever he picked up turned out to be something he didn't want to listen to. He couldn't define just what would sound good to him just then, but no more could he find it on the radio.

He hit a newscast once and stayed with it all the way through, waiting for an item about Ferris even though he knew there could not possibly be one. There had to be more men killed each day in Texas than the radio stations had time to tell you about, particularly radio stations in Oklahoma that wouldn't likely be that interested in dead men turning up in Texas pastures.

Of course he'd left the corpse jaybird naked, which might give it a little more in the way of news value. How often did they find a naked man with his head bashed in in the middle of nowhere? Damn, he thought, that was an intriguing question, and he had no idea at all of the answer. Ten times a day or once a year or anywhere in between, as far as he had any way of knowing.

He had never killed a man before.

He thought about it and wondered how true it was. When you tended to move around a lot it was hard to be sure whether you'd left a man dead or not. A couple of times he had had to cut somebody or other, and having done so he had had to get the hell out, and two men at least had taken cuts that might have bought farms for them. And when you hit a man over the head and grabbed his roll and took off down the street, you never did know if maybe you'd hit him harder than you might have meant.

And there had been times, too, when a couple of hours had gone by and he'd emerged later on with no clear notion of just what had happened in the course of them. When you had a lot of speed in you and tried to come down with booze and reds, sometimes your mind had an anxious trick of slipping back on itself and coming at you on the blind side, and you would wash out a chunk of your memory as clean as a peeled egg, and what you did then you never would recall. Sometimes such moments seemed to come back in dreams, and he would claw his way out of sleep trying to snatch the dream out of the air and hang onto it, but you'd as well grab smoke.

He didn't like those lost hours. Lately he had learned to avoid them. You had to take the speed edge off slowly, carefully, with a little wine or cough syrup and a couple of reds, and as soon as you had turned up into down you had to crash, had to get quickly into a bed and under the black hood of sleep. It was fighting the reds that wrecked you, because if you tried to operate under the Seconal instead of letting it take you out, then your body kept working and your brain went into another room and your memory was like a tape recorder with the microphone unplugged; the wheels went around but nothing was registered. Whenever he awakened to a memory lapse he left whatever town he was in, because there might be a reason he *had* to leave, and that possibility was always reason enough.

His long-term memory was spotty and unreliable, but this did not much trouble him. When you moved around a lot, when you never took time to put roots down, it was only natural that you didn't clearly recall what month or what year, what town or what women or how they all fit together. And if you stayed in front of things and on top of things, if you put both feet in the present instead of living in the past and dreaming on the future, you couldn't waste time remembering things that had no importance for you. You'd be wasting part of your mind, a part that could better occupy itself with more important things.

Like the fact that he had killed a man and left him naked in a cornfield. Correction — a pasture. His mind kept wanting to call it a cornfield because it sounded better, but facts were facts and brush and dry grass was all that field had held.

He had killed a man, for the first time that he could swear to, and now he was trying to decide how he felt about it.

The sky was red to his left when he saw the deer. Red and gold, with the sun dropping just a little below the dark-blue sun visor, and he was still on 281 and still in Oklahoma when damn if there wasn't a big buck deer standing smack in the middle of his lane. He hadn't seen that deer come out. It was just nowhere at all one second and in front of him the next, and he didn't panic or sweat, just held onto the wheel and put the brake pedal on the floor.

The big car fishtailed a little and stopped fast enough so that he felt the pressure of the seat belt against his middle, and of course there was no goddamned deer at all, nothing in front of him but blacktop, and thank God nothing behind him because anybody tailgating him would have run halfway up his ass the way he stopped that thing.

No deer at all. No deer now and no deer in the first place, and he got off the brake and onto the accelerator and coaxed the Toronado back up to a nice steady sixty miles an hour.

A few miles back he'd stopped at a diner

to use the toilet, and he'd considered dropping another bennie at the time. He'd decided to wait awhile, and now he was glad of it. Because while it was no big deal to see an occasional deer who wasn't there, or a car or a person or a shadow, it was a clear enough sign that it was time to let things spin out a little on their own, time to pull the pin and let the spool unwind.

He drove past the first motel, drove for a quarter of a mile, then turned around and came back. It was a way to leave the impression that he was coming from the north and heading down toward Texas, but by the time he made the turn he realized it was a waste of effort. Because nobody in the motel would notice which way he had come from, let alone attach enough significance to it to remember it when some policeman turned up in a month or a year.

Something to guard against, he thought. There was just no sense in being *too* smart. Not with other people as dumb as they were. Just doing the things that mattered was as much as you had to bother with.

The motel was a U-shaped building of concrete block, with the office in back at the bottom of the U. There were a dozen rental units on either side of it. The concrete block had been given a wash with a rusty shade of pink that was starting to fade where the sun hit it the most. The doors and window trim were blue, just a shade darker than the Toronado. There was a small swimming pool in the center of the complex, and he thought he might have a swim until he noticed that the water had a green scum on the top of it and the sides of the pool were stained with algae. He thought of going to another motel, not for the sake of swimming now but because a motel with no pool at all was preferable to a scummy one. But he just didn't want to drive any more just now, not with the roads filling up with deer that were there one minute and gone the next.

If the room was dirty, he'd simply leave. It wasn't costing anything anyway; the vacancy sign had four smaller signs hanging from it, indicating the credit cards that were honored there, and Walker P. Ferris was three for four.

The man behind the desk had rimless glasses and cheap false teeth. He looked as though he knew the paint was fading and the pool scummy but just couldn't bring himself to do anything about it. His flesh had shrunk around the cords in his neck. When Jimmie John asked for a single he said, "Rooms are twelve dollars, all the same price." He said it as though he had been saying it twenty times a day for fifteen years.

The room was cleaner than he had expected. There was a band of paper over the toilet seat and the water tumblers were sealed in plastic wrap. The water had an iodine smell to it and he knew it wouldn't stay down, but he felt the urge to retch and drank a glassful and threw up carefully into the toilet. His mouth and throat tasted strongly of bile. He drank another glass of water and repeated the process and felt better.

He took a long deliberate shower and scrubbed himself thoroughly. He got his razor and shaving soap from the Delta Airlines bag and shaved until there was no stubble, not even against the grain. He used the last of his after-shave lotion and dropped the empty bottle in the plastic trash basket.

Also in the flight bag was a four-ounce bottle. The label said it contained elixir of terpin hydrate and codeine, that if drowsiness occurred one should avoid driving or operating machinery, that the preparation might be habit-forming, and that persistent coughs should be brought to the attention of one's physician. The bottle was a little more than half full. He drank about an ounce of the mixture, at first grimacing automatically at the awful taste of it, then enjoying its warmth in his throat and stomach.

He tried to recall just where and when he had obtained the flight bag. He knew he'd had it a couple of months, and that he had acquired it in a bus terminal while its owner was standing on a ticket line. But he couldn't be sure where the terminal was or what the owner had looked like. He did remember that the owner was female, because the bag's contents had consisted primarily of unwashed stockings and underwear. A disappointment, that — he'd hoped to find something useful, and wound up quickly discarding everything but the bag itself.

And he'd probably be getting rid of it, too, before long. It was cheaply made and one seam was already starting to go. Well, he had Walker P.'s suitcase in the car trunk. He'd have to have a look at it soon. Have to see whether it, or anything inside it, would be useful. Have to get rid of anything that wasn't.

But not just now, thank you. Chores could wait. He still had to wash out his socks and underwear so they'd dry by morning, and maybe wash his shirt, too, if he felt ambitious. But not just yet.

He stretched out naked on the bed and let the air-conditioner finish the job of drying him. He closed his eyes and let his hands take inventory of his body. He located an ingrown hair just above his right knee and sat up for a moment to attend to it. He lay flat again, eyes open, staring sightless at the ceiling.

The cough syrup, added to his own exhaustion, was taking command of the amphetamine he had been taking all day. His mind was starting to spin free and loose now. Even with his eyes open, his retinae were screening a haphazard stream of pictures, the random fragments of waking dreams. He saw a furious montage of sharply delineated faces, faces of people he had never seen in life. It wouldn't go away. He could turn it off completely for awhile, but he couldn't fix on one particular face and try to hold onto it for a long close look. The faces were like the dreams he tried to clutch at on awakening. Like grabbing smoke.

He thought about going out for something to eat. And decided nothing was worth leaving the room for, and certainly not food, which he would almost certainly not hang onto anyway. Better just to lie here, he thought, and then he stopped thinking entirely.

About an hour later he blinked several times, took a deep breath, and got out of bed. He washed his socks and shirt and underwear and hung them up to dry. He had the flight bag unzipped, ready to shave again, before he remembered that he had shaved earlier. He did run his hands over his face, though, to convince himself that shaving was truly unnecessary.

And then he had to unzip the flight bag again anyway for the reds. There were not many left, and he would have to remember to score some soon.

He took two, drank a glass of the foul water, and went right to sleep.

MODERATOR: *In other words, Dr. Rasmussen, you see these tragic occurrences as symptomatic of some of the flaws in our social structure? Could you comment further on that for our radio audience?*

RASMUSSEN: *Certainly. We have evolved into a highly mobile society. This mobility has been attained at the expense of a solid and permanent social structure. Our youth grow up with a sense of infinite possibilities, and at the same time with a lack of roots. Nothing is established, nothing is predetermined. The young person owes no allegiance to family, to community, to society at large.*

HEGLER: *I wonder if I could comment on that?*

MODERATOR: *Dr. Hegler.*

HEGLER: *I wouldn't presume to take*

issue with Dr. Rasmussen. Certainly the decline in the nuclear family and the lessening importance of the tight-knit community have been not without effect. But these alone do not explain individual outbursts of violence.

RASMUSSEN: I was merely attempting to put this incident in a social context.

HEGLER: Yes, of course. My point is that the particular pressures upon the individual may do more to tell us why one member of society turns to violence while another does not. In this particular instance I think we would do well to look to our old friend, the Oedipus complex.

RASMUSSEN: Oh, not that again.

HEGLER: Yes, precisely that again, and in the case at hand, the subject suffered from the absence of a strong and permanently established father figure toward whom rebellion could be focused. His mother, from what we know of her, had a succession of casual partners. No doubt the boy's attitude toward his mother, as well as toward these temporary father figures, was ambivalent. Ultimately he would select a female partner who could function symbolically as a mother while masking this capacity by inexperience and permissiveness. His hostility toward the family unit as an entity, which found such vivid expression, can be perceived as hostility toward his own family background, a background he always sought to escape but could never entirely outrun.

RASMUSSEN: *If I may?*

MODERATOR: *Dr. Rasmussen.*

RASMUSSEN: *I wonder if Dr. Hegler and I are not saying much the same thing. The simultaneous desires to return to one's roots and to wholly uproot them engender a conflict which can be resolved only by —*

FOUR

When she came downstairs her parents had already finished breakfast and her grandmother was still asleep. It seemed to Betty that the family always ate in shifts. All four of them were rarely at the same table at the same time.

There was half a glass of orange juice left in the carton. She poured it, drank it standing at the refrigerator, rinsed out the glass and set it in the sink. She scrambled an egg, toasted a slice of bread. There was no milk, but then she didn't much care for milk first thing in the morning, and her father wouldn't let her drink coffee. He had never explained his opposition, and the one time she asked him about it he wound up launching into a tirade against her sister Judy. "She was a one for drinking coffee," he had said, "*and* smoking cigarettes, *and* running with the boys. The Whore of Babylon gone to hell in her short skirts. And

69

look at her now. Just you look at her now."

She ate her eggs and toast and drank a glass of water. Her parents drank coffee and fought. As usual, it was hard to tell what the fight was about. There didn't seem to be any particular point in contention. The two of them took turns reciting familiar lists of the other's failings.

"House needs painting and the porch won't never be fixed and the yard's all mud. . . ."

"Married you and never knowing I was getting your mother in the bargain. Old woman with her teeth in a jar and her mind out in a wheatfield somewhere. . . ."

"Jobs you had and can't keep a one of them. I swear I should have married Eric Josenhans. Twenty years now with the same company and Susan drives around now in a brand-new Camaro and I can't begin to tell you how much that boy thought of me. He worshiped me, he never would of took up with Susan Harb but for me not seeing him for dust, blind as I was at the time. . . ."

"Way you take care of this house. Buy you a dishwasher and you'll stack the dirty dishes in it and not have the sense to turn it on. Just let 'em sit there so's you've got another storage place for dirty dishes. . . ."

"Mother always thought the world of Eric. And he was polite to her. . . ."

"Not much point keeping the house clean with the old bitch stinking it up like she does. She could die tomorrow and this house would stink of her for the next ten years. Not a chair I can sit in without that smell coming up at me like poison gas. I tell you and tell you, let her sit in her chair and nobody else's, but for all the good it does to tell you a solitary damn thing. . . ."

It was all the same as always, and she sat there and listened to them, wondering if they ever took the trouble to listen to each other. It was hard to believe that they did. Nothing either of them said ever got a noticeable reaction from the other. They just went right on delivering their lines. The tones of their voices never varied. They spoke with very little expression, and yet their conversation must have had more meaning to them than you would guess from the monotones in which they conducted it.

Because it was not entirely directionless. Sooner or later one of them would mention her sister Judy, and though everything beforehand might have been ignored, Judy's name was instantly recognized as a signal for the second round of the fight.

And in this round they were always more or less on the same side, the two of them united against the absent Judy. There might still be a certain amount of infighting — *"You were always too strict with her." "You let her have her own way too much, spared the rod and spoiled the child."* But these were asides, never permitted by either party to derail the conversation from its ultimate objective, the utter condemnation of Judy as the spawn of the devil, and a gathering of forces for the third and final round, which consisted of a discussion of Betty's recent behavior and an analysis of what she must and must not do to avoid following in Judy's wayward footsteps.

"And this one, Frank."

"Oh? What about her? Not that I expect it's something that will bring me joy."

A long sigh from her mother. "I just don't know about her. I tell her and tell her to come right home after school —"

"Where were you yesterday, Betty Marie?"

She explained again how she had been studying with Carolyn.

"Studying?"

"There's a Spanish test this morning."

"And what's the matter with studying by yourself in your own room?"

"It's better if you study with another person. You take turns, you know, one of you asking the words in English and the other answering them in Spanish, and that way it stays in your mind better. The teacher said —"

"Teacher say it always had to be the other girl's house you study at?" He squinted at her, his eyes small and mean. He was a high school athlete gone soft, big in the belly, flabby in the upper arms. He was still strong, though. Once he and a friend had been working on a Volkswagen and didn't have a bumper jack that was suited to the little car, and Frank Deinhardt had lifted the back end of it and held it while his friend got one tire off and the other one on. Then he'd been two hours getting his breath back completely, but that didn't take away from the fact that he'd picked up one end of a car all by himself.

He went at her some more. "One thing," he said. "You could be helping more around the house. And you could do your own studying and let this Carolyn Fischer do hers. Or do the two of you do a little more than studying?"

"What do you mean?"

"All innocence, aren't you. Never you mind what I mean. School's out at three o'clock, today you be home by twenty minutes past."

"I can't."

"Then three thirty, but —"

The movie, Robert Redford and Cybill Shepherd. "I can't," she said again. "I have to stay after school."

"What-all for?"

"Mr. McCulloch said I had to. I've been having trouble with algebra and I might fail it —"

"With all the studying you and Carolyn Fischer do?"

"— and he wanted me to stay in yesterday for special help, but I told him how we had to study for the Spanish test, so he said it could wait a day if I would promise to come in today, so I said I would, and I can't put it off another day because —"

"Who's this teacher again?"

"Mr. McCulloch," she said.

"Algebra."

"That's right."

"You were always good at arithmetic."

"Algebra's different. And this is intermediate algebra, logarithms and everything, and it's harder. More complicated."

"*Mr.* McCulloch."

"That's right."

"And he wants you there after class. After everybody else goes on home. Just you and him in an empty classroom."

She saw her mistake now. Why couldn't she have said Miss Culver or Mrs. Skirm or Miss Tuthill or even made up a name? Mr. McCulloch had come to mind because he was the teacher most likely to keep her after class, poorly as she was doing in algebra, but she should have realized it would be a mistake to mention any male teacher. Her father would have offered objections to a female teacher as well, but he would never have voiced them so strongly.

He said, "I know about those old men. Old schoolteachers, and everybody thinks they're respectable as the First National Bank, and then they get some dumb little girl off by herself. Those old men."

"Mr. McCulloch's not old."

"Oh?"

"He's about twenty-five," she said, and then saw that this was only making it worse. "Or thirty, maybe. But not what you'd call old."

Her mother and father exchanged

glances. Her father said, "You ever stay after school with *Mis*-ter McCulloch before?"

"No."

"You positive, Miss?"

"No, I never did. I —"

"You be home this afternoon by three thirty. Hear?"

"But I promised —"

"Then you break that promise, hear? Goddamn you, don't you have the sense God gave a goose? Do you want to wind up a round-bellied whore like your sister Judy? Do you want to be a tramp that has to leave town and never come back? Is that the kind of name you want for yourself, Miss?"

Yes! Yes, that's just exactly what I want. To be like Judy. To get out of this place and never have to see it again, and never have to look at you again, at any of you, at any of the people in this town, to be out of it once and forever and never come back, yes, that's what I want.

"No," she said.

"You be home by three thirty."

"All right."

"You tell that arithmetic teacher he has to send home a note before I give my permission for you to stay late. You watch how he changes his tune. Meantime you come straight home and help your mother around the house."

"I will."

The Spanish test was easy. After class she heard some kids moaning about how hard it had been, and she couldn't understand it. She had only had to stop and think on one word, "dangerous," and even then she had remembered almost immediately that it was *"peligroso."* The other words she'd gotten right without even thinking.

And of course she had made no spelling mistakes. Many of the other students frequently misspelled words in Spanish, and she found this incomprehensible. Anyone could spell things wrong in English, but Spanish was set up to make such errors impossible. There were a few rules to learn and then everything was clear; if you heard a word you could spell it, and if you read a word you could always pronounce it correctly, because the rules worked without exception. There was a sentence in her textbook: "Spanish is a completely orthographic language." She liked that word, "orthographic," and she liked the concept it embodied.

You would think all languages would be orthographic. It would make life so much simpler for everyone. Of course, it would put a lot of spelling teachers out of work. And you couldn't have any spelling bees in a country with an orthographic language.

She imagined herself trying to explain a spelling bee to a native of Madrid. "But *Señorita,* they stand there and take turns spelling words aloud? *Son asnos!*"

In her other classes, as she sat daydreaming and writing her name in her notebook, she spent a lot of time thinking about Spanish. The concept of spelling bees appealed greatly, and she elaborated mentally on a conversation concerning them. She tried to conduct both sides of the conversation in her head. Her vocabulary was not really large enough for all her thoughts on the subject, and the glossary in the back of her Spanish text failed to fill in all the gaps.

It was funny how she was so good in one subject, so interested in it, and so poor at and bored by the others. She even enjoyed being called on in Spanish class. Words came quickly to her then, and the nervousness that was otherwise a part of such moments was not present when she spoke in

Spanish. Perhaps because she was speaking in a language not her own, and thus it was as though she were talking in another person's voice.

It was interesting to think about these things. It was more interesting than what was being said in her other classes, and it was less disturbing than thinking about what she would do after school.

She wanted to go to that movie.

Suppose she said that Mr. McCulloch had insisted. He had told her that she was in grave danger of failing algebra, and that he would not have time for her later in the week, and an hour or two of private instruction could clear up all the problems she was having, and —

No. It wouldn't work. The more intense she made Mr. McCulloch's arguments, the more her father would become convinced that Mr. McCulloch had ideas about her that had nothing to do with equations and logarithms. And if she made enough of a thing out of it, her father might even decide to confront Mr. McCulloch and demand an explanation, and if that happened she would have the choice of admitting her lie or brazening it out and hoping he would decide to speak to Mr. McCulloch right after he fixed the porch and painted the house, which would leave her safe for the next twenty years.

And even if he believed that Mr. McCulloch compelled her to stay, and even if she found some way to convince him that her algebra teacher was not a threat to her virginity (by intimating that Mr. McCulloch was queer for boys or something, but doing it carefully, because it would upset her father to learn that she had any information on such topics) he would still be furious with her for choosing to disobey her father rather than her teacher.

She had promised to go straight home.

But she couldn't bear to go straight home. She wanted to see that movie.

If she went to the movie, she couldn't possibly be home before six o'clock. The movie would start at three thirty — they always did, to accommodate kids from school — and with the coming attractions and all it would last two hours at the least, and by the time she got home it would be six or close to it. Maybe there was something she could invent to account for being two and a half hours late. Normally this would not be much of a problem, but the morning's discussion had put an edge on things.

She would have to go home. The movie would still be playing the next day, and she could see it then.

But —

When the last bell rang she dawdled at her locker, purposely delaying the inevitable. At last she walked out the front doors and down the steps. The sun was as bright as it had been yesterday, the sky as clear and cloudless.

As she approached the front walk, a car pulled to the curb alongside two girls who were standing and talking. She recognized them — both seniors. The car was not one she had noticed around town before. It was very distinctive, an Oldsmobile Toronado with the body painted in an unusual shade of blue and a gleaming white vinyl top. She couldn't see the driver's face, but saw him lean across the front seat and say something to the two senior girls.

She saw them exchange glances and giggle, and one of them said something and the driver said something in reply, and they giggled again, and one of the girls shook her head. The driver straightened up behind the wheel and the car pulled off.

She followed it with her eyes, thinking that she could have made up a whole story about the car and the person driving it. She watched as the car slowed several times, finally stopping a hundred yards or so down the street. After a few seconds the door on the passenger side opened and a girl got in. She was too far away for Betty to recognize her.

She went on watching as the car disappeared from view.

Texas license plates. All the way from Texas that car had come, and a girl walking home from school had caught the driver's eye, and now they were riding off together. He would take her off and make love to her and they would never see each other again. Or he would drive her home to Texas to meet his parents, stopping en route at a Justice of the Peace to marry her, and he would present her to his mother and father and they would embrace her and welcome her into the family, and —

And the girls who had giggled and shook their heads would have made a decision that would change their lives forever, and never know what they had missed.

She knew, suddenly, that she was not going home. She was going to see that movie.

She walked quickly to the theater. It was

never crowded on weekday afternoons. She would be able to sit surrounded by empty seats, entirely unaware of the dozen or so other people who would be in the audience, wholly wrapped up in the movie itself.

And then she would emerge from the theater when the film ended, unless it was good enough to justify sitting through a second showing. In any event, she would sooner or later leave the theater, and she would then go directly to the bus station and buy a ticket for as far away as she could afford. She would not need a return ticket because she would not be returning. Ever.

Except that she wouldn't do it. She knew that much before she even reached the theater. She would want to, and it was fun to think about it and plan it, but she would not be able to do it. Instead she would eat a box of popcorn, and maybe a couple of candy bars and a Coke, and she would watch one showing of the movie and go straight home.

By then she'd have a story worked out. If it was just her mother at home she might have a chance. If her father was there, well, she was going to be in trouble.

She bought her ticket and went inside.

Now living next door to them, of course it's a strange feeling. Something like this happens and you look back on it and try to see all the reasons why it would be them and not somebody else.

I'd see him a lot because he'd spend a good amount of time out front working on his cars. Sometimes I might have a beer with him to be sociable. Just a man like everyone else as far as I could see.

She kept to herself pretty much, but then so did he, except that he'd be outside more. Far as the daughter, I recollect seeing her walking to and from school but aside from that I haven't any real impression of her.

The other daughter, she was gone before we moved here. We lived over on Monroe Avenue up until three years ago. Never knew there was *another daughter.*

You look for reasons and you could

make some up, but like as not they'd be no closer than wild guesses. Far as I knew they were people like anybody else on the block. Good people, I would say, but they could as easily have been bad people and I'd not likely have known the difference.

My wife's people are religious, and they'll have an explanation for everything, but to me it's like one person gets struck by lightning and the one standing next to him doesn't and you're wasting your time figuring it out.

FIVE

He awakened very abruptly that morning. He sensed there had been a dream shortly before waking but remembered none of it. He got quickly out of bed, showered, shaved, combed his hair. He was packing the flight bag when the nausea hit him like a fist.

At first he fought it, but not for long; he had learned the futility of that course. He forced himself to drink water and forced himself to throw it up. He drank a second glass of water and leaned against the beige sink until he knew it was going to stay down. Then he dropped a bennie and finished packing.

Good weather outside, and a fresh clean taste to the air. He felt like running. At fourteen he had tried out for the school's cross-country team. At first he had liked it — jockstrap and sneakers and little white cotton shorts and T-shirt, running for an hour or two over red dirt trails, pitting himself as much against the distance as against the boys he ran with. And the good ache afterward, the tiredness that went beyond the muscles and into the bones. The fierce appetite for dinner on days when he had trained. The deep sleep he fell so easily into on such nights.

He hadn't made the team. You never did, not your first year. Five boys ran for the school, and he was about eighth on the list, and sure to be selected the following fall.

In the spring he went out for track, but it was not the same. They didn't even run the mile at his school. The longest race was the 880, half a mile, and he had no real speed at short distances. The training itself bored him. It didn't extend you like distance running. Instead you just did the same fool thing over and over again, fighting a clock instead of a distance. He dropped the whole thing after a couple of weeks.

And when fall came around he was into other things and never even showed up for the first training session, and that was the end of that. It was later that year that he'd dropped out of school and never gone back, and by the following autumn he didn't even live in that town anymore.

But he would still think about running once in awhile. He might be in a car and pass a passel of runners strung out along the shoulder of the road, and the feeling of that earlier autumn came back flashing. Sometimes he wanted to urge those runners on, and sometimes he envied them, and sometimes he wondered why in hell a man would want to run when he could ride.

There were no great bonanzas in Walker P. Ferris' suitcase. Of the clothing, only the socks fit, and he had no powerful urge to wear another man's socks. He found two pairs of cuff links which might be worth pawning, although he doubted it, and a bottle of after-shave lotion he found he preferred to his own brand. He thought of discarding the clothes but decided it would be easier for the time being to leave them in the trunk.

Before he drove off, he took two towels from the motel room, soaking one of them in the sink. A mile down the road he pulled onto the shoulder and gave the car a quick wash and dry. He tossed the towels into the brush and drove off.

North through Waynoka and Hopeton

and Alva and across the Kansas line. A stop for breakfast just over the state line, a hamburger and home fries and a cup of coffee with three packets of sugar stirred into it. The food was greasy and the smell of years of frying hung in the air, but this time he didn't mind it. Sometimes he did and sometimes he didn't.

When he left the diner a guy and a girl were admiring his car. He flashed on punching the guy out and riding off with the girl, imagined her scared but excited at the same time, sitting next to him with her eyes darting around like a little rabbit, while he just kept driving and didn't say a word. The picture appealed, and his hand moved involuntarily toward his back pocket. Then the girl turned a little and he saw she had buckteeth and a chin full of acne.

He walked to the car and opened the door. The girl smiled over the hood at him. He returned the smile, then gave the same smile to her boyfriend, a long drink of water wearing paint-spattered jeans and a homemade haircut.

The guy said, "Some car."

"Gets me where I'm going."

"From Texas?"

"Galveston. Well, just outside of Galveston."

"Long way from home."

"Long way to go."

"Where you headed?"

"Oh, a lot of places." He got into the car and the guy came around and stood by the window before he had time to zip it up.

"This the baby with the front-wheel drive? How do you like it?"

"Every car ought to have it."

"Is that right?"

He nodded, pushed the button to raise the window. The guy was saying something else but he pretended not to hear. He pumped another smile at the two of them and got back on the road.

The girl hadn't said a word. He thought, *Too bad you weren't a little better looking, lady. We might of gone for a spin, just the two of us.*

North across the uncompromising flatness of Kansas. Medicine Lodge, Pratt. At Great Bend he crossed the Arkansas River. A little farther on he crossed the Smoky Hill. The traffic was light and the car was a pleasure to drive, cruising effortlessly over the straight and level road. Endless grainfields punctuated by little towns you were in and out of without noticing their names.

Space. Endless space. If your eyes were good enough you could see to the end of the world.

Brief pit stops at roadside places in the middle of nowhere. A gravel road would cross the highway and somebody would open up a gas station on one corner and somebody else put a diner on one of the other corners, or maybe a general store. Quick stops for gas, for a Coke, for cellophane-wrapped crackers spread with peanut butter and cheese. Then back in the car and back on the road and north again.

Russell. Luray. Osborne. Roadside signs shouting at him, telling him to visit Jewell County State Park, to stop at the Wayfarer's Rest Motor Lodge, to drink Dr Pepper, to prepare to meet his God. Eat, drink, go, buy, stay, see —

The signs kept turning into voices. People wouldn't leave you alone. You got in your car and closed your windows and sat back and drove and they still had to yammer at you. Do this, buy that. Of course you could turn off the signs the same as you turned off conversations, you could let them go right through your eyes and out the back of your head.

Smith Center, and 281 joined up with

36 and headed east. U.S. 36 was a better road but it was taking him east, and after about seven miles 281 cut north again. He almost missed the turnoff; shutting out signs, he shut out the road sign as well. He spun the wheel, cut off a trailer truck and was rewarded with the blast of a horn.

Another handful of miles and he was out of Kansas. A sign told him Nebraska welcomed careful drivers.

Across the Republican River and up through Red Cloud and Cowles and Blue Hill. Between Ayr and Blue Hill a jackrabbit came out of the brush and onto the road in front of him. He swerved to miss it but the rabbit sprang the wrong way and took a wild bounce off the left front fender.

He screeched to a stop, threw the car into reverse. He found the rabbit a few yards off the road. The animal was not at all bruised or bloody, and the only thing wrong with it was that it was dead. He picked up the soft carcass and held it for a moment, then set it down very gently in the roadside brush and ripped up handfuls of grass and weeds to cover it. Tears welled up behind his eyes and he felt a wave of dizziness coming at him. He closed his eyes and tightened his hands into fists and took deep breaths until everything straightened itself out.

He got back into the car and just sat there for a few minutes. He unlocked the glove compartment and took the gun out. He spun the cylinder a few times. Then he put the gun back and relocked the glove compartment and drove on.

Fields of wheat and sorghum. Vast open plains, with no trees but those clustered around the farmhouses or lining the streets of the few towns. Towns like Hastings and Doniphan, and then the North Platte River, and finally a town called Grand Island.

He had been thinking off and on about the girl with the buckteeth. Her face kept getting mixed up with the face of the dead jackrabbit. It was more, he decided, than the obvious similarity of the teeth. There had been a rabbity quality about the girl, although he had not recognized it as such at the time.

He did not often think about girls. The ones he had known had always been a disappointment to him, although it was difficult to say just how or why they had failed to come up to his expectations. He did not know exactly what those expectations were.

He did know, though, that there would someday be a girl who would be right. Such a girl existed. He was sure of this, and just as sure that their paths would cross when the time was right. He was in no hurry for this to happen. Like everything else, she would come when the time was right, not before and not after. Things always came when it was time for them to come. Like the car.

Sometimes at night, when the uppers were wearing off and the downers just starting to hit, he would sing love songs that he made up spontaneously by himself, both words and music. He did not try to hold onto these songs. Sometimes, while singing softly to himself, he would recognize a bit of melody or a string of words as something he had employed before, in one or a dozen earlier songs. But he never took the trouble to polish a lyric or carve a melody line into finished form because he was not sufficiently interested.

Grand Island. He drove around, wondering where in the hell the name had come from. They called it Grand Island, and as far as he could make out it wasn't either. Flour mills, canneries, packing plants. Stockyards, evident to the senses from blocks away, and houses built unbelievably close to them. He wondered how a man could live so close to a stockyard, how he could breathe that stink day after day.

It was early afternoon, but he knew that he was done driving for the day. That rabbit had bothered him. Ever since he hit it he'd been driving slowly and braking at shadows.

And there was that other rabbit that he couldn't get all the way out of his mind.

Buckteeth and pimples, and an expression on her face that did a lot of nothing for him. So if he still kept thinking of her that meant it was time for him to get himself a girl.

He found a motel, took a room. He showered again and changed his socks and underwear. He drove around until he found the town's main business street — which wasn't all that hard to find. He walked around a little, had a Coke and a piece of apple pie at the lunch counter in the five-and-dime, bought a pair of shoes and two pair of socks at the Florsheim store, bought two shirts and a pair of pants and a plaid double-knit sport jacket at Kleinhans Menswear. He used up a lot of old Walker's cash money, but now that he had the man's suitcase it only made sense to get something to put in it.

He did some more driving. Around two thirty he passed the high school. He made a point of driving past it again fifteen minutes later, but still saw no signs of activity. He came by again just after school let out and drove once around the block, making a quick recon of the girls and letting his mind play around with attitudes and opening lines. Next time around he slowed down, pulled up next to two girls who were standing and talking, hit the button to drop the window.

One had dark-brown hair; the other's hair was just a shade lighter than his own. The brunette was the prettier of the two. She wore a black-and-white checked skirt and a lime-green sweater. There were freckles on her cheekbones and across the bridge of her nose. The other girl wore a dark-green skirt and a white blouse. Her breasts were unrealistically pointed. Her face was sour; you could see already the woman she would become, dyspeptic with the little injuries life kept inflicting on her, always bitterly resigned to continual dissatisfaction.

To the brunette he said, "Now what's a girl like you doing outside on a beautiful day like this? You should be spending the afternoon all cooped up in an air-conditioned car."

They looked at each other and giggled. The brunette said, "You're not from around here, are you?"

"Texas. But I'm around here now, so this is your lucky day."

"You sure think a lot of yourself."

"Now why should I go against the tide of public opinion?"

They giggled again. It was not his favorite sound in all the world.

"Hop in," he said. "We'll go for a ride."

"Both of us?"

"Just you. This here car doesn't seat but two people."

"I can't just leave Diane like that."

"Sure you could. Diane here's a big girl."

"You could drop me at my place," Diane offered.

The brunette thought about it, then shook her head. He had the feeling he could talk her into it without a great deal of trouble, but he also had the feeling that she wasn't worth the bother. Girls always disappointed him, and he expected as much, but she had disappointed him already without even getting in the car.

"Suit yourself," he said, "but you'll purely never know what you're missing."

He raised the window before she could answer, drove slowly on down the street. He paused from time to time to check out what was available. A lot of the boys and girls he passed took a lot of notice of the car.

He didn't lower the window again until the car was alongside a slender blonde with an armful of books. She didn't look at him, but when he stopped the car she stopped walking, and when he leaned across the seat toward her she turned to face him.

He said, "I wonder if you could give me some directions."

"Where to?"

"Well, what I'm looking for is a pretty blond girl who wants to go for a ride."

She grinned and turned even prettier. Blue eyes, and good clear skin, and what looked like a good body. He could tell her legs and ass were nice — she was wearing rust-colored dress jeans and filled them perfectly. Her white blouse was cut too generously to give him much information about her breasts.

"I don't guess you'll have much trouble finding what you're looking for," she said. "Not with that car and that line."

"Could be I already found what I'm looking for."

"Could be I got a boyfriend."

"Wouldn't surprise me in the least. Girl like you ought to have a lot of them."

"Just one. A *steady* boyfriend."

"I got an old hound dog back home. I guess he's as loyal as your boyfriend, but that doesn't mean I let him tell me where to go and who with."

"Just a ride."

"That's all I offered, seems to me."

"Well —"

He opened the door. She got in and closed it, and the seat belt signal buzzed at them. She had a little trouble hooking the belt but he let her work it out for herself.

She said, "He'll kill me if he finds out. Well, he can use a little shaking up." She lit a cigarette with the dashboard lighter. "Where do you keep your hound dog, anyway?"

"Sleeps at the foot of my bed."

"I mean where do you live, silly."

"Texas. Just a little town called Houston."

"Oh, one of those rich Texans."

"Not me."

"Oh, sure. Lots of poor boys have cars like this."

"They would if they had rich daddies."

"Is your father rich? I bet he's got six oil

wells in his backyard."

"Not in our backyard, but a few more than six. I don't suppose you ever heard of the Westfield Oil Company?"

She was so obviously impressed that he wondered if maybe she *had* heard of the Westfield Oil Company. He never had himself, but that didn't necessarily mean there wasn't one.

"And he . . . owns it? It's his company?"

"Preston Ferris, President. That's what it says on his office door."

"And your name is —"

"Walker P. Ferris."

"What's the *P* for?"

"To keep the Walker from bumping into the Ferris. No, it stands for Preston. My daddy's name is actually George Preston Ferris but he doesn't use the George. It's an old family name, Preston."

"My name's Emily. Emily Morgan."

"That's a pretty name."

"It's so ordinary, though." She laughed suddenly, and he asked her what was so funny. "Oh, I was thinking. My steady's name is Stuhldreier. Don Stuhldreier. If, oh, if we were to get married, my name would be Emily Stuhldreier."

"Wouldn't be so ordinary that way."

"The thing is, I don't know if I want to

be named Emily Stuhldreier. Emily Morgan Stuhldreier. But to expect a man to go and change his name on your account —"

They went on talking, but although he kept up his end of the conversation he stopped paying much attention to it. She was already starting to muse on how Emily went with Ferris, he knew. But not aloud. Instead she was telling him what her father did for a living — there were no oil wells in Mr. Morgan's backyard, sad to say — and what funny thing one of her teachers had said that morning, and other bits and pieces of information he had no deep and abiding interest in. No doubt she was popular, and her friends thought of her as a good conversationalist. He'd have liked her conversation more if there had been less of it.

She said, "Where are we going, anyhow?"

"I don't know. Just driving around, having a look at the scenery."

"You make a left just past that next house and then a right about two miles down and there's a real pretty road. It's quiet there, and, you know, private."

After they made the right turn she asked him what had brought him to Nebraska.

"My daddy wanted me to look at some property in Oklahoma," he said. "Then I was going to head back home, and I decided I wanted to get off by myself and do some thinking."

"About anything in particular?"

"Oh, about getting settled down."

"You're young for that, aren't you? How old are you?"

"Twenty-four."

"I'd have said twenty-two at the most. That's still young."

"Well, my daddy's been sick. I guess he'd like to see me settled before he goes. Wouldn't mind seeing a grandson born, far as that goes."

"Oh, I'm sorry he's ill."

"He's a wonderful man."

"I can imagine. Is there a . . . girl back home in Houston?"

"Not for me there isn't."

She fell miraculously silent. They passed a white farmhouse set close to the road on a slight rise of land. A black and white cow was tethered to an oak tree in the front yard. There were half a dozen chickens scratching in the gravel driveway. He drove for another quarter of a mile and cut the engine. She showed just a trace of a smile as the car coasted to a stop.

She said, "Well, Mr. Walker Preston Ferris."

He couldn't think of her name. "Well," he said.

He unhooked his seat belt. "I'm having trouble with this," she said, and he leaned over and unfastened her belt. He felt her warm breath in his ear. He started to straighten up, and their eyes met, and he kissed her.

He could taste the cigarette in her mouth, but he went on kissing her. She began to breathe a little faster. He put a hand on her breast and felt her. Her breast was larger than he had thought it would be. It filled his hand nicely. She responded to his touches, then drew a breath and sat back.

She said, "Oh, my."

He reached for her. She hesitated for a second, then let him draw her into his embrace.

She was foolish and talked too much, and he didn't like her cigarette breath, but she would do. He kissed her and felt himself responding to her and knew that she would do. He put his hand between her thighs and stroked the crotch of her jeans. "You're awful fast," she said, but that was all she said and she offered no resistance.

When he started to unbutton her blouse, she drew quickly away and rebuttoned the top two buttons. "Someone might see us. It's broad daylight. It would be different at night."

"There's nobody around."

"Cars come by every once in awhile. Here, let me do you, it'll be okay."

Her hand was in his lap, fingers quick and certain with button and zipper. She drew him out and held him in her hands.

"You'll see," she said. "You'll like this." And her hands moved skillfully.

Desire died like a felled ox. He felt it going, felt himself softening, and a red flame danced at the back of his brain. He wanted to kill her.

He took her by her shoulders and shoved hard. She went reeling backward and struck her head on the window. Her mouth fell open.

"Get out," he said.

"I thought you would like that."

"Get out."

"If I did anything wrong I'm sorry. I thought you would like it. Most boys —"

"Get out of the car."

"Look, I said I was sorry." She inched tentatively toward him. "I really like you, Walker. I'll do whatever you want. You can take my clothes off if you'd rather. I know a place we could go."

"Out."

"Or I'll suck you off if you want. I never do that but I'll do it for you if you want." Her hand reached for him and he slapped her hard across the face.

She put her hand to her face. Quietly she said, "You had no call to hit me."

"You silly little whore. Get out of the car."

"You can drive me back. You can leave me off where you picked me up. It doesn't matter."

"I'm not driving you anywhere."

She stared at him. "Are you crazy? Do you know how many miles —"

He took her throat between the thumb and forefinger of his right hand. He said, "I could kill you. Is that what you want?"

She must have read it in his eyes, must have realized suddenly that he was speaking the literal truth, that he very easily *could* kill her. Because her face changed and there was real fear in her blue eyes. She kept her eyes on his and reached behind her for the door handle, fumbling until she found it. When the door opened behind her he gave a shove and she tumbled out of the car.

"You bastard!"

He reached across, drew the door shut.

"You fucking bastard! You dirty son of a bitch!"

He flashed on a scene: lowering the window and leaning across with the gun in his hand, and her eyes widening in terror when the gun came into view, her curses chopped off short by her fear. And she would back off, her eyes filled with the gun, and he would wait until she turned and started to run, and then the big gun would buck in his hand and she would crumple up and fall.

"Bastard! Dirty cocksucker!"

He pressed the button on the glove compartment, then remembered that it was locked. Instead he turned the key in the ignition and drove off down the road.

He kept going until he found a driveway to turn around in, then sped back toward her. By the time he reached her she was halfway to the farmhouse. She was walking awkwardly as if she had hurt her leg when he threw her out of the car.

He slowed down. She turned, and he honked the horn at her and put the accelerator on the floor. The tires kicked up a spray of gravel. In the mirror he watched her shake her fist at him. He put his head back and laughed.

He drove back into town, drove around a little, slowing down now and then when he saw a girl walking alone. None of them appealed enough to tempt him to stop the car.

At a drugstore he had a small Coke. As soon as he finished it he asked where the men's room was. The waitress directed him. He went downstairs and down a long aisle with cardboard cartons on both sides. It took a great deal of effort, but he managed to master the nausea until he was in the lavatory. Afterward he rinsed his mouth thoroughly, went back upstairs and had a dish of strawberry ice cream. The waitress, a gaunt woman with a wedding ring, flirted lightly with him. He didn't take her up on it. He ate a few spoonfuls of his ice cream, washed a bennie down with a glass of carbonated water, and left.

At five twenty he was approaching the Orpheum Theater just as the show was letting out. He had given up looking for a girl by then. But he saw a girl emerge from the theater with a book bag over one shoulder and a particular expression on her face that he seemed to recall without ever having seen it before.

With no hesitation whatsoever he pulled the car over to the curb and lowered the window.

"I could tell you something nobody knows. Nobody in the world."

"What?"

"But if you ever told anybody —"

"I won't."

"I mean I would just about die."

"I won't tell."

"If you ever did —"

"Oh, come on, Emily. Didn't I tell you what happened with Kenny?"

"This is a lot more than anything that ever happened with Kenneth Fuhrmann, believe me. I shouldn't tell anybody, not even you."

"Well, then, forget it. If it's such a big deal."

"That's just what it is. A big deal."

"Look, either tell me or don't tell me."

"I just don't know."

"If you don't want to —"

"Oh, I want to. Of course I want to. You

promise you won't ever say anything?"

"I already said —"

"I'm just so scared. All right, I'm going to tell you. I was in the car with him."

"Who?"

"You know who. Him. Jimmie John Hall."

"You're kidding."

"I am not kidding. He drove right past the school and he stopped the car for me and I got in."

"I know he tried to get Diane Bishop and Patti Stryker to go for a ride. You can't talk to either one of them without hearing all about it. But they wouldn't go and then he drove away."

"No he didn't. He drove on down the street and stopped for me. Nobody saw, thank God. If Don found out he would kill me. Or if my father found out. God, if you ever tell anybody —"

"I said I wouldn't. What happened? My God, I can't believe it. You actually got in the car? What was he like?"

"Very good-looking. Very smooth, you know? Nicely dressed and he had a real cool way about him."

"God, Emily. Why did you get in?"

"Well, I don't know. It was a hot day and I didn't feel like walking."

"You're really wild."

"Well, I didn't know who he was. Or what he was like or anything."

"What happened?"

"He started driving. And then he headed out of town."

"Were you scared?"

"Course I was. Because I started to get a feeling, if you know what I mean."

"That he was going to try something?"

"More than that. He was strange."

"Tell me about it. What did he say? How did he act?"

"Oh, I don't know exactly. He was just strange. I got a feeling like, I don't know, like I wouldn't be able to stop him if he tried something."

"What did you do? You must have been scared stiff."

"I was. What I did, I tricked him. I got him to stop the car by pretending I would cooperate, if you know what I mean. Then the minute the car stopped I yanked that door open and ran for my life. I just ran like crazy across a field."

"Did he come after you?"

"He started to. And I knew he would kill me if he caught me. I just knew it."

"God!"

"But I kept running and when I finally

looked back the car was gone. I guess he didn't feel like running all over a field on a hot day. Maybe he was afraid he would get his clothes dirty or something."

"If he caught you —"

"If he caught me, I wouldn't be here today."

"Oh, my God. How did you get home?"

"Got a ride with a farmer. I was almost afraid to get in his truck, I was afraid to get in anybody's car or truck, but I couldn't walk all the way home. I rode back to town with one hand on the door handle, believe me."

"And nobody knows? You never told anybody?"

"Not a soul. I didn't know there was any- thing to tell at first. And then when I found out I was just terrified. I'm still scared, if you want to know."

"I believe it."

"I wake up in the middle of the night wanting to scream. I can still see him coming out of the car after me."

"You were lucky."

"You said it. When I think what could of happened. Listen, you won't tell anybody, will you?"

"Never."

SIX

At first she did not believe it was happening.

The movie had completely enveloped her. It was a story of doomed young love, and at the end when she watched Robert Redford die and then saw Cybill Shepherd turn magically from girl to woman as the light drained from her eyes, she was too intimately involved in what she had seen to cry. She was, at that moment, a part of the movie, and she was still deep inside the movie as she left the theater.

And then, incredibly, that car was waiting at the curb for her. The blue Toronado with the white vinyl top, its window descending, its driver leaning toward her, his eyes alive and full of her. The movie had been so utterly real that she could only assume that this was a continuation of movie-reality, that it was not actually happening at all.

She waited for him to say something. When he remained silent, she opened the door and got in beside him. She closed the door and buckled her seat belt and he put the car in gear.

She said, "I saw you two hours ago. In front of the high school. You talked to two girls and drove down the block and another girl got into your car."

"I didn't see you."

"No. I was halfway up the steps. I didn't really see *you*. Just the car."

"If I had seen you then —"

"My name is Betty. Deinhardt."

"Jimmie John Hall."

"Would that be Jimmie or Jimmie John? That people call you."

"I don't know that people call me anything. I don't talk to people. Jimmie John."

"Jimmie John."

"Would you like a Coke or something? I don't know the town. Name a place and we'll go there."

"Where I ought to go is home. What is it, five thirty? I was supposed to be home two hours ago. But I wanted to see that movie. I could have waited and seen it tomorrow. I thought of that, and then, I don't know, I didn't want to wait. I don't like to wait for things."

"Neither do I."

"It was a fantastic picture. Do you go to the movies much?"

"Once in awhile."

"You ought to see it. God, he's gonna kill me."

"Your father?"

"He's a bastard. He really is. They had this huge fight this morning and the two of them turned it all on me. How I had to be home right after school because they don't trust me. That's such a laugh you wouldn't believe it. I mean, nobody ever bothers with me. Girls, boys, nobody. I'll go days without even talking to anybody."

"You just move here recently?"

"I was born here. I just don't, oh, I don't know. I think he's crazy. My father. I mean it, I think he's crazy. Six years ago he drove my sister out of the house and I've never seen her since. The only person who ever cared about me. And now the two of them talk about her and call her a whore and then turn on me. Do you want to know something? *I hate them.* I mean it. I never said that before, not even to myself. It's true. I hate them."

"My parents are dead. My father before

115

I was born, and then my mother a few years ago."

"I'm sorry."

"You don't have to be sorry. And I lied to you, or maybe I didn't. My father could be alive or dead and I wouldn't know. He ran out on my mother before I was born. *If* he was ever with her. She said they were married, but how would I know? So maybe I'm like your father."

"Huh?"

"A bastard. Look, I don't want you to get in trouble. Do you want me to take you home?"

"Yes, I guess you better. The longer I stay the worse it's going to be. No."

"How's that?"

"Can I change my mind? I don't want to go home."

"Sure."

"We could drive past there if you'd like. So you can see where I live. Do you want to? You turn where that car is turning, only left instead of right. My sister was not a whore or anything like that. They're both completely crazy. She was a wonderful person. I think she's a stewardess now, or possibly a nurse. I think about seeing her someday, and other times I think I'll never see her again."

"Take it easy, Betty."

"I'm all right. It was the movie, and talking to you. I can never talk to people. I'll have the words in my head and they just stay there while I stand around like a re-tard. Her name is Judy. My sister."

"Do you have any other brothers and sisters?"

"Make the next right turn. That building is where I used to go to grammar school. Brothers and sisters. No, only my grandmother. She sits all day in front of the television set and . . . passes gas. What's so funny?"

"The way you said it."

"It's all she does. I mean it. She never talks to anybody and never pays attention when you talk to her, and I know it's because she's so old and everything and she can't help it, but it's really disgusting. One more left turn, not this corner but the next, and we're just about there. Another thing, she sits around with her teeth out. She has false teeth but won't keep them in her mouth. Sometimes I think she just does it to be revolting."

"I don't have anybody. Listening to you, maybe I'm better off."

"It's that house right there. No, don't stop, Jimmie John. Just keep right on going. I don't even want to slow down. He's home. But even if he wasn't I wouldn't go in there now. Do you want to know something? I am *never* going back. I just decided that this minute."

"You'll change your mind."

"Do you really think so? No, I won't. All I think about lately is getting out of here. This place. 'This fucking town.' I don't talk that way. That was what Judy called it the night she left. I'm not going back. I'll get on a bus or something. Or hitchhike, except it's supposed to be dangerous because you don't know who you're riding with. Did I say something funny again? The way you smiled just then."

"Well, I've thumbed rides from time to time. I was just thinking."

"You must think I'm crazy. Talking a blue streak like this and I've never seen you before. It just seems natural."

"I don't think you're crazy. I think —"

"What?"

"I think we oughta get something to eat. Where's a good place?"

"There's a restaurant across the street from the Orpheum. The movie house where we met. Where you picked me up, I guess you would say."

"Where we met."

"That was nice. Do you want to know something? You're a very nice person."

"Oh, now, you're dead wrong about that."

"I don't think so. Do you know the way back? You want to turn left, and then —"

"I know the way back," he said.

At Rinaldo's they shared a booth and ate grilled cheese and bacon sandwiches and French fries and drank coffee. She set her cup in the saucer and leaned an elbow on the formica tabletop. There was a Waylon Jennings song on the jukebox. The singer told how he'd left town after a love affair went wrong, and now he was

. . . Gonna spend the rest of my life
Not comin' home to you

She said, "You'll never guess how big a thrill this is for me. I mean having coffee. I'm not allowed to drink it at home."

"Why not?"

"It's all tied up with being a whore like my sister. I don't smoke or wear makeup so they can't put their foot down about that, so they made a rule that I'm not allowed to drink coffee. 'This fucking town.' I'm not going to say that any more. I don't

119

like the way it sounds, coming from a girl. And you don't like me to say it, do you?"

"Let's just say I'm glad you're not going to say it any more. I'm glad you don't smoke or wear makeup."

"You are?"

"But you can drink all the coffee you want."

"Could I have some more? Thank you."

"Did you really mean it? About not going back home."

"I meant it. I *still* mean it. I should've left before this." She looked at her coffee cup. "Only I'm glad I didn't leave before today."

"So am I."

His hand covered hers. It was the first time he had touched her. She raised her eyes to meet his.

He said, "Do you have a boyfriend? Anything like that?"

"I told you. I don't have anybody."

"Because I'd like us to be together."

"Do you mean that?"

"Yes."

"I feel like crying. Don't worry, I'm not going to. I don't cry much. I can't believe this. I don't mean I don't believe you. But all this. That it's happening."

"Finish your coffee."

I'm gonna spend this Saturday night
Not sittin' home alone
And I'm gonna spend tomorrow
Not callin' you on the phone

They both liked: country music, hours just before dawn and just after dusk, holding hands. They both hated: sloppiness, cruelty to animals, people who talked but couldn't listen. They were in the car, driving on back roads south and west of the town. The sun was down, the sky already quite dark. The car radio played the same song they had heard in the restaurant.

And so I walk that narrow line
Not stayin' good and true
And I'm gonna spend the rest of my life
Not comin' home to you

The song echoed and echoed in her mind. It was a song a man would sing to a woman who had wronged him, but to her it seemed that Waylon Jennings was singing it for her, to her parents. She was going to spend the rest of her life not returning to that house, to this town. No matter what happened, she was not going back.

She did not know what would happen.

So far, what had happened could have more easily happened in a dream. Except that in her dreams fulfillment was never quite within reach. Her most frequent dreams were of two sorts. In one, she was naked in public places, very intent on getting from one place to another, and never quite able to cover herself properly. People would stare at her and turn away, annoyed with her for appearing nude before them. In her other standard dream, she was trapped someplace very high and had to descend steep staircases and clamber over treacherous catwalks and narrow ledges. She never actually fell, but neither did she ever accomplish the descent, for each staircase led to another ledge, each catwalk to another suspension bridge or rope ladder, and the bottom was never within reach. So no, this was not like any dream she had ever dreamed, but it had the insubstantial quality of dreams.

And if she had not dreamed this, she had certainly entertained it in fantasy. It was not merely that he was the nicest boy she had ever met, nor that he was obviously pleased with her and happy with her company. More astonishing than that, more literally fantastic, was that she became in his presence a different person. Indeed, she became her own self. She was able to talk to him. She could speak words and thoughts that had previously been locked up inside her. And, at times like this, she could be silent, they could both be silent, while he drove with one hand on the wheel and the other in hers and she leaned back and closed her eyes and the interior of his car became all she knew of the world.

"Why do they call it Grand Island?"

"What do you mean?"

"The town. It's not very grand —"

"You know it."

"And it's not on an island, as far as I can see."

"Oh. No it's not, but — which way did you come into town? From the south?"

"Came up on 281."

"Well, you know where you cross the North Platte? You cross it once and then you have to cross it again? That's the island. It's, I don't know, forty or fifty miles long. That's the grand island that the place got its name from."

"But that's a pretty good piece south of here, isn't it?"

"Uh-huh. But there's no town on the island, so they fastened the name on the nearest town they could find. Except it's not the nearest."

He started to laugh and she laughed with him. She said, "There are a lot of names like that. My high school's a new building, and the blackboards are green because it's supposed to be better for your eyes. And they write on them with yellow chalk. But they still call them blackboards."

"When by rights they should call them greenboards."

"Right! Only nobody ever does, and nobody ever notices how silly it is. Or they'll talk about drinking out of a plastic glass."

"And if it's plastic it's not glass. Let me think. Oh, I knew a man once who would talk about this old hound dog of his, and he'd say, 'I tell you, that coon dog of mine is a real son of a bitch.' "

"People don't even think what they're saying."

His hand tightened on hers. "People don't think what they're saying, or what they're doing, or much of any damned thing. I'll tell you something. I don't care much for people, the bulk of them."

"Neither do I."

"They don't know how to use their minds or their bodies or their lives. You can just walk right through them. Do you know what I mean?"

"I think so."

"Sometimes I think I'm, oh, I don't know." She waited. "I think sometimes that I'm different from everybody else in the world," he went on. "That I can do just about anything I want by concentrating, by using myself properly." He laughed suddenly. "Now just hear that old boy carry on! Lord, don't he give a person a powerful earful."

"I like when you talk like that."

"Southern, you mean? I guess I always talk like that, don't I?"

"No. Your voice and all changes a lot."

"I guess I sound like where I've been. And I've been all over, one time or another."

"And I've never been anywhere."

"Well, you got time."

She wondered if he would take her with him. They were not going anywhere now, just circling around, enjoying the car and the evening and each other's company. But in the morning she would leave town, and she thought it not impossible that he would want her to go with him. She was certain they would not be together very long, because she could not believe he would want her for very long, but she could accept that. She felt wonderful while she was with him. She would settle for that for as long as it lasted. And, when he did not want her any more, she would at least be far from Grand Island and out of the state of Nebraska and on her own. The hard part, she knew, was getting out in the first place. Once she was gone, it would be very easy never to return.

. . . I'm gonna spend the rest of my life Not comin' home to you

"I have a room."

They were back in the town again. It was turning cool, and he had put the heat on low. She looked out the window. A couple of men had a car up on a jack and were busy changing a tire. In a doorway, an old man was drinking something out of a paper sack. Halfway down the block, a part-shepherd dog trotted off the curb and turned to stare at them, its eyes flashing red in the beam of the headlights. Jimmie John slowed the car, braked to a stop. The dog went on regarding them for a few moments.

He said, "That's okay, dog. We got all the time in the world."

The dog stayed still for another moment,

then trotted briskly the rest of the way across the street, tail wagging.

"Now that dog," he said, "is a real son of a bitch."

"He wasn't afraid of us or anything."

"Oh, he knew I'd stop for him. I was saying. I have a room, it's in a motel. Do you know, I don't remember the name of the motel. I've got the key in my pocket, I expect it has the name on it. Doesn't matter. I know where it is."

She didn't say anything.

"You could stay with me tonight. If you wanted to."

"All right."

He was silent for a few moments. Then he said, "The name I took the room in, it's not my name."

"Oh."

"The name I told you is my own. But I have these credit cards; they have another name on them. So if I put that name down I can use the credit cards and it doesn't cost anything."

"That's really neat."

He looked at her sharply for a moment, then grinned. He said, "That's what it is, all right. The room, well, I don't guess it's too bad. What's important is it's clean."

"That's the important thing, I guess."

"Betty? You can just sleep. What I mean is, I won't bother you if —"

"If what?"

"Well, if you don't want."

She squeezed his hand. She didn't say anything, and neither did he.

She had prepared herself to walk with perfect nonchalance past the desk clerk, but, as it turned out, there was no need; Jimmie John drove around the side of the motel and parked in front of the door to his room. He opened the door with his key, flicked on a light, then stood aside so she could walk into the room ahead of him.

"Oh, it's very nice," she said.

She had expected to be very nervous and found herself at ease. If anyone was nervous, he was. He was so completely sure of himself that his lack of assurance now was very touching. Soon he would take her in his arms. He would kiss her, and they would make love.

Of course she would not be as good as the girls he was used to. But he liked her, she knew he liked her, and that would make up for some of it.

He said, "I guess I'll take a shower. Unless you want to go first."

"No, I'd just like to sit for a minute."

"There's a thing there for making coffee, if you want some. You just fill that little pot with water and put it on the coil, and the weight of it makes the coil heat up. And then there's instant coffee and sugar and cream and a stick to stir it with, all wrapped up in a little package."

"I don't think so. If I have more coffee now, I won't be able to sleep."

"Maybe in the morning."

She looked at him, and his eyes slipped away. He went into the bathroom, closed the door.

Now he's taking his clothes off, she thought. And then she heard the water running in the shower.

She got on the bed but couldn't sit still. She moved around the room, touching things absently. There was a large portable television set on one end of the dresser. It was bolted in place to prevent theft, as were the various table lamps, but was mounted on a swivel so that you could watch it from any part of the room. She switched it on, but before the picture could come into focus she switched it off again. She did not want another presence in his room. *Their* room.

Should she undress and join him in the

shower? Did he expect her to do that?

But if it was not what he expected, if in fact it was not what he wanted, it would be an awful mistake on her part. And then it occurred to her that perhaps he did not want her at all. That he wanted to be with her but did not want her sexually. The thought disturbed her in ways she did not completely understand.

She heard him turn off the shower. A few moments later the bathroom door opened and he emerged with a towel fastened around his middle. He was tanned nicely, and his chest was smooth and hairless. Her father had body hair like an ape and would sit around on summer nights in sleeveless undershirts, drinking beer and perspiring heavily, scratching at the roll of soft fat on his belly. There was no fat on Jimmie John's body. She saw now that he was leaner than she had realized, slender and wiry.

When she passed him she caught the scent of his after-shave.

"Don't be too long now."

"I won't."

"There's just the one lever in the shower. You want to adjust it to the right position before you get under it, or it comes on too hot or too cold."

When she had showered and dried herself, she wrapped a towel around her so that it covered her from her breasts to the middle of her thighs. She couldn't fasten it but held it with one hand behind her back. She studied her face in the mirror. She had never considered herself pretty, but she did look pretty now. Would he think she was pretty?

Instinct made her put out the bathroom light before opening the door. He had turned off all the lights but one bedside lamp. He was under the covers. She moved toward him and studied his eyes and the planes of his face.

She dropped the towel. She looked at him and his eyes were full of her. He said her name. She closed her own eyes and was briefly dizzy. When she opened them he was reaching to turn off the lamp. He drew back the bedcovers for her and she got in beside him.

He said, "You're beautiful."

"Oh, I am not."

"Come here."

When he kissed her she thought she was going to die. She had imagined a thousand equivalents of this moment. But it was much more than she had ever imagined. His body against her and his mouth on hers — it was more than she had thought it could be.

He kissed her for a long time. She put her arms around him and felt the weight of his upper body upon her breasts. He kissed her eyes and the tip of her nose. He lay beside her and rested a hand just below the curve of her breast. She put her own hand atop his and interlaced their fingers.

"I don't know anything," she said.

"We don't have to do anything."

"I *want* to. But I've never been with anyone."

"Don't be afraid."

"I'm not afraid. Just tell me what to do."

"Just lie still."

She lay there, breathing slowly and deeply, and he began to make very gentle love to her. Slowly and tentatively his hands learned the contours of her body. He touched her breasts, her legs, between her legs. For a long time she did not feel anything that could be properly labeled excitement. His mere presence was excitement in itself, and the novelty of lying open to this boy, of being touched by him, was thrilling.

Then, before she knew it, she began to become passionate. Something extraordinary welled up inside of her. She thought she was going to burst open. Her heart was racing. She could not get her breath. She walked catwalks and narrow ledges, and instead of falling she soared.

"Oh, God!"

"Easy," he said. "Easy, now."

"It was so beautiful." She turned to him and tucked her face into his shoulder. "Oh, I love you, I love you."

She must have slept then, because when she opened her eyes he was sitting in a chair by the side of the bed. He was wearing a pair of white cotton under-shorts.

He said, "I was watching you sleep. You looked like a little kitten."

"That was so wonderful. But it was —"

"What?"

"All for me. I want to be good for you."

"It was good for me."

"You know what I mean."

"Don't worry about it."

"Is it because I'm a virgin? I don't want to be a virgin. Not now. I'm glad there was no one before you but I want to . . . do everything. With you."

He leaned over and kissed her. "You sure are impatient," he said.

"I mean —"

"One perfect hell of an impatient virgin.

Don't you know we got all the time in the world?"

"I do love you."

"Why, I guess you better. Don't know what I'd do with you if you didn't."

She grinned. Then her face went serious again. "Isn't there something I can do?"

"Like what?"

"*You* know."

He kissed her again. "Didn't I tell you all the time we've got? Now I have to go out for a little while. I have to see about something. You take a little nap until I get back, hear?"

"I don't know if I can sleep. Can I come with you?"

"Not this time. I won't be long."

She watched as he dressed. She just loved to watch him, loved the easy grace with which he moved. Before he left he came over and kissed her again. "Just like a little kitten," he said, and she made a purring sound and he laughed softly.

She lay in the bed, her head on the pillow, her eyes squeezed shut. If he didn't come back —

But he would come back, of course he would. She fastened on the thought and sleep caught her by surprise.

No, I never suspected anything like this.

To tell you the truth, I never thought much about having a sister back there. Once I was gone I just never looked back. I had a life to make for myself. It hasn't been easy, I'll say.

I don't suppose I gave much thought to the idea of her growing up. She was just a little kid to me, like she stayed the same age in my mind as she was when I moved out. I don't suppose she even remembered me or thought much about me if she did. And I would guess they poisoned her mind about me if she thought about me at all.

I've got kids of my own now, and the hours Roy works and all, believe me, it's a handful. I've got all to do to take care of my own life.

I feel terrible, of course, but it's like

something you read about in the papers. It doesn't touch me. I feel bad, but I can't feel that it touches me.

We were never close.

SEVEN

It was just too perfect the way things were falling into place. First the car and now the girl. And all just as he had known it would be.

Damn, but he was just completely on top of things! The wrong car had come and he had known to wait for the right one, and he had not had long to wait. And then the wrong girl had come and he had thrown her out of his car and out of his life, and drove around looking for nothing, nothing at all, and sure enough the right girl walked out of a dingy movie house in Grand Island, Nebraska, and into his life.

And he kept knowing what to do. That was the amazing part of it. He had stopped early in the day in Grand Island. There was no reason at all to stop there, except that he had by God *known* it was the time and the place.

Years of moving around, years of

waiting, and all the time knowing that somewhere out there was the other half of himself. And every time he'd found a girl he'd been disappointed, until he had known in advance to expect disappointment, but still in the back of his soul there was always the ache for the right girl, the perfect girl, and who would have guessed he would find her here?

And, remarkably, he had found her at the precise time when she was ready to be found. Ready to move out, ready to pull up stakes, ready to grab at a new life. Ready to belong to somebody, and the somebody she was ready for was Jimmie John Hall, and it couldn't be plain and simple luck because there was no such thing. You couldn't get by on luck. Nobody could. You got by on drive and push and edge. You stayed on top of things and on top of yourself, and you were always ready, and everything broke right for you when the opportunities came along.

Of course she might disappoint him. So far everything about her had been right, so incredibly right that it stunned him. The soft unreached cleanliness of her. The tone of her voice. The way she set her head when she listened to him, and her way of hearing both the words he said and the

words he did not say. And what *she* said —
he could actually listen to everything she
said; he had no need to tune her out or
shut her off.

If she did disappoint him —

But he was not going to think about that
now.

The sounds she made. The way she softened and melted beneath his hands. The
way she let go and was so utterly his and
became more completely herself in the
process.

Looked like a little kitten when she slept.

Hard to believe anyone could sleep with
another person in the room. He himself
had to be alone in order to sleep. But she
had dropped off in his arms, her face moist
against his chest, and she had not stirred
when he disengaged himself and got out of
bed. She went on sleeping like a warm
little kitten while he sat in the chair
watching her. And he could have gone on
watching her all night.

He might even be able to sleep with her
himself.

He backed the car out of the parking
space, drove out of the lot and circled carefully around the town. While his woman
lay trustfully sleeping, he would have to

provide for her. He needed money. There would be two of them now, and with her at his side he would have to stay in decent places and eat in decent restaurants. He couldn't expect to use the credit cards much longer. By now, even if no one had turned up Walker P. Ferris' body and identified it as such, surely someone had begun to wonder what had happened to old Walker. There would be a missing persons' report filed if there hadn't been already, and there would be a notice out about the car. He could hold the car for a little while longer, but he would have to figure on paying cash from now on.

The last pill he had taken had worn off, but he still felt as if he were coasting on a speed run. He stopped for a traffic light, eyed the Sunoco station on the far left corner. Not everybody used credit cards. Gas stations still took in a certain amount of cash.

A while ago he had taken forty dollars off an Exxon station. Where? It might have been in Valdosta, Georgia. It seemed to him that he had been through there about the same time as he hit the Exxon station, but he couldn't be sure. He remembered the incident itself well enough, though. He'd stopped there late at night to use the men's room and noticed on his way back to the highway that there was only one attendant on duty, an old man who kept dozing at his desk. And so he had given the man time to doze off again and then crept around the station from the back. He could readily picture the old man at his desk, the underarms of his dark-green work shirt soaked with sweat, the roll of fat on the back of his neck, the empty coffee container and half-finished sweet roll on the desk before him, the moths buzzing furiously in the light of the yellow bulb they supposedly couldn't see.

One little tap on the back of the head with his piece of pipe. That was all it took. The old man had started to stir even as the pipe was descending, as if warned by instinct, but it hadn't done him any good. One little tap and he was stone certain of a few hours of sleep, and the cash box yielded a stack of ones and fives and a single ten, and it all added up to forty dollars.

The light turned and he crossed the intersection. This Sunoco station was no good now. It was on a busy corner, there was a car at one of the pumps, and there looked to be at least two attendants on duty. No point in taking that much of a chance.

Of course you had to take chances. If Walker P. Ferris hadn't been willing to take chances he'd still be pumping gas for his father-in-law. Funny how things all fitted together — gas stations and old Walker P. and everything else, like a song that started on a certain note and wandered all up and down the scale and came back to the same note at the end. Well, Walker P. Ferris had taken that chance, and look how lucky he was.

At another traffic light he cut the ignition, unlocked the glove compartment, then started the engine again.

He found the right station out on 281 north of the city line. It was a Standard station. There were no lights anywhere near it, no customers present. He pulled up to the pump and cut the engine. Might as well get some free gas while he was at it. The tank was better than half full, but it wouldn't hurt to fill it the rest of the way.

The kid on duty trotted out right away. He was beefy, and his belly bulged against the front of his denim shirt. No more than nineteen or twenty, but you could see he'd be jowly in a couple of years.

Jimmie John lowered the window and told him to fill it with the high-test. While the gas was running he worked on the windshield and made conversation. "Allaway from Texas, huh? This here a Toronado? How you like it?"

He gave him a credit card. The kid went back inside to do whatever they did — check it in the book, run it through the machine. Jimmie John opened the glove compartment and took out the gun. He wedged it under his belt, opened the car door, stepped outside.

On the highway a couple of cars passed without slowing down. He grinned. Business wasn't very good, he thought, and it was about to get worse.

He went into the station. There were vending machines for coffee and Coke and cigarettes. A wire rack had pockets for eighteen road maps, but all but three pockets were empty. There was a calendar on the wall from a sparkplug manufacturer. The page for that month showed a fisherman netting a trout.

The kid was at the desk struggling with the credit card machine. He said, "Sorry to hold you up but I can never get the hang of this thing. Ruin two slips for every one I get right. You want the men's room, it's locked, key's on the wall there. I don't know why the hell they lock it."

Then he looked up and saw the gun.

He said, "Oh, Jesus. Look, all I do is I work here. It ain't my money and no skin off my butt. Ain't much in the register but you're welcome to it."

But the kid had seen him. And the kid had seen the car, knew the make, knew it was carrying Texas plates. And the kid knew the Ferris name from the card.

Maybe he had made the decision far in advance. But he made it for sure now and the kid saw it in his eyes.

"Jesus, no," he said. He started backing away, little tentative shuffling steps. "No, no," he kept saying. His little eyes seemed to draw even closer together. He was trying to look Jimmie John in the face but his eyes kept dropping to the gun as Jimmie John leveled it at him.

A man had to take chances if he was going to amount to anything. But this stupid fat kid was just giving up, standing there whimpering with his hands out in front of him to knock the bullet away.

He squeezed the trigger.

It wouldn't work. He said, "God damn it," and tried to force it. A safety catch, he thought, and he turned the gun furiously in his hands searching for it.

And through it all he thought what a poor dumb helpless piece of shit this old

144

boy was. Because he was standing there waiting to get shot and blubbering like a girl while Jimmie John stood there obviously not knowing what in hell to do with the gun. He just stood there while he could be picking up something, a piece of pipe, a wrench, an ashtray, anything to defend himself with. He saw all this and thought of all this, and then his fingers finally found the damned safety catch and flicked it off.

And the kid was still standing there like a statue.

He smiled. Not purposefully but automatically, and the kid saw the smile and something died in his eyes. Finally he readied himself to spring, but it was a whole lot of seconds too late, and Jimmie John squeezed the trigger and this time the action was just as it was supposed to be and the bullet went home three inches above the navel.

Damn, but did that gun have a hell of a kick to it! He fired a second time reflexively, but by then his arm had jerked half out of its socket and the bullet ricocheted wildly off the ceiling. The kid was sprawled against the wall with his legs straight out in front of him. He had his hands clamped over the wound in his middle. His shoulders were twitching and his mouth worked soundlessly.

Jimmie John shot him in the chest. The recoil was just as strong this time but he was more nearly prepared for it. Even so, his arm ached. He took two steps and pointed the gun very carefully. A muscle worked in his forearm. He waited until his aim was steady and pumped a final slug smack into the middle of the kid's forehead.

He rang the cash register, scooped out all the bills, left the silver. The little tray with his credit card had dropped from the desk. He picked up his card and pocketed it. Halfway out the door he remembered the credit slip. He took it out of the machine.

He put his gun back in the glove compartment and locked it. Then he drove back to town.

He didn't feel it at first. Not until the car was back in his parking place in front of the motel room. Then it began to hit him. He killed the lights and ignition and leaned forward against the steering wheel. He closed his eyes and flashed the whole sequence from the moment he walked into the station.

He had never felt like this before. He

couldn't define it or break it down but he knew he had never felt like this in his whole damn life.

If she wasn't in the room —

But she had to be in the room. He told himself this and ordered himself to relax. He could manage to will the tension away, but seconds later it was back, more demanding than before.

He unlocked the door of the room and went inside. He reached for the light switch, then let his hand drop to his side. He let his eyes accustom themselves to the darkness.

She was in their bed. A sleeping kitten, her body curled like a question mark, her hands clutching her pillow. He took a deep breath and released it slowly.

He had gone out, a hunter after prey, and he was returning now from a successful chase. And his woman was in their cave waiting for him.

He undressed in the darkness, moving silently to avoid disturbing her. He did not trouble to hang his clothes up but folded them neatly on an armchair. He went to the side of the bed and looked down at her while his loins burned painfully with a fierce need for her.

She moaned quietly when he lowered

himself onto the bed. But she did not awaken. He lay quietly beside her for awhile.

He took hold of her shoulder. It was just wonderful how soft she was. He rolled her easily onto her back. She made a sound he had never heard before, half protest and half purr. He nuzzled her throat, moved to kiss her breasts. The tempo of her breathing changed. He put a hand on her belly and ran it down to her loins. His fingers opened her thighs and touched her.

She was all warm and wet.

He placed himself in position over her. The intensity of his erection was painful. He touched her moist warmth with it and clenched his jaws to keep himself from surging furiously into her. He moved just a little ways into her and her eyes opened.

"Oh, God," she said.

He did not move.

"Oh, do it, *do* it. I want you to."

He drove into her. She sobbed and her arms tightened around his back. He made himself move slowly, gently, but it was impossible to do so for long, and then she was moaning his name and moving with him and he moved fast and hard, fast and hard, and when he came it was like a gunshot.

"You wanted to see me?"

"Yes, doctor. I understand that Mrs. Ella Hall is a patient of yours?"

"Could I ask your interest in the matter?"

"I'm sorry. My name is Carstairs, I'm with the Associated Press."

"Yes?"

"I wonder if it would be possible for me to see Mrs. Hall."

"We have no Mrs. Ella Hall here."

"I was given to understand —"

"I assume you mean a Miss Elizabeth Jenks."

"I mean the mother of James John Hall, but I believe 'Jenks' was her maiden name. She's a patient here?"

"She is."

"Would it be possible for me to see her?"

"I'm afraid not. Miss Jenks cannot have visitors. In any case, you would find her unresponsive."

"If I could just observe her —"

"I'm afraid that's against policy."

"Could you tell me anything about her condition?"

"I don't see why this would be of interest."

"It's good to be able to give our readers a full picture, doctor. There's a great deal of public interest —"

"Yes, there always is, isn't there?"

"If you could just —"

"Miss Jenks has been officially diagnosed as schizophrenic, catatonic type."

"Could you put that in layman's terminology, doctor?"

"Oh, shit."

"Sir?"

"It isn't layman's terminology you want. What you're after is something sensational. Something scary that will please your most gruesome readers. Something to sell papers."

"Doctor, I. . . ."

"Skip it. Miss Jenks has to be fed with a spoon. Miss Jenks pisses in her bed like an infant. She hasn't said a word since she was admitted to this hospital."

"When was that?"

"Three years ago February."

"Would you say she's a human vegetable?"

150

"I would say she's suffering from schizophrenia, catatonic type. If you'll excuse me —"

"Doctor, would it be your opinion that her son's behavior might have been responsible for her mental condition?"

"It would be my opinion that you're trying to put words into my mouth."

"I merely asked —"

"I know what you asked. Look, dammit, we know hardly anything about schizophrenia. We don't know what causes it. We don't know for certain what it is. It may be a biochemical imbalance, it may be hereditary, it may be any of a number of things. Miss Jenks displayed obvious symptoms shortly after the onset of menopause. Whether the illness was related to menopause I cannot say. Whether she was emotionally ill beforehand I cannot say. I understand her son left home some years before she was hospitalized."

"You mentioned something about heredity, doctor. Is it possible her son inherited a predisposition toward mental illness?"

"That would call for an assumption concerning the nature of her illness that I am not prepared to make. It would also call for an assumption concerning her

son's mental condition."
"Would it be possible to say —"
"I'm afraid that's all for now."

SAY JIMMIE JOHN
MIGHT HAVE INHERITED
MENTAL ILLNESS FROM
HIS MOTHER

EIGHT

She awoke to the sound of him gagging in the bathroom. It was a horrible sound.

She said, "Jimmie John? Honey?"

He didn't answer. She got out of bed and walked toward the bathroom door. She called his name again and he told her not to come in. She heard the toilet flush, and then he was sick again, and the toilet flushed a second time. She sat down on the side of the bed with her hands on her knees.

When he came out she said, "Are you all right? I'm worried about you."

"Nothing to worry about."

"Are you sick?"

"I just get nauseated sometimes. Especially in the mornings. Like first thing in the morning before I have any breakfast in me."

"Should we get dressed and have breakfast?"

"Not just yet," he said, and smiled, and she felt his eyes on her body. His gaze warmed her. He sat down beside her and moved to kiss her but she turned her face aside.

"I didn't brush my teeth yet," she said. "You don't want to kiss me."

"Well, I do want to kiss you. And other things. Go brush your teeth."

"Actually, I don't have a toothbrush."

"You can use mine. 'Less you're afraid of catching something."

"If there's anything you've got, I wouldn't mind having it."

"You brush your teeth and you're more than welcome to it."

He was waiting in bed for her when she returned. She was excited the minute he put his hands on her. No — she had been excited before then. All it took was a glance from him and she wanted him. He was slow and gentle with her now, and she reached orgasm twice before he put himself into her. She came a third time the instant he was inside her and a final time, most powerfully, when he finished. That last time was like drowning, and she closed her eyes, and when she opened them he was seated on the chair again, watching her.

"Did I do it again? Fall asleep, I mean."

"Just for a couple of minutes. More like passing out than fall asleep."

"Do I look different?"

"What do you mean?"

"Not being a virgin. I looked in the mirror before but I didn't notice anything. Do I look any different to you?"

"Not a bit."

"What's so funny?"

"Oh, just thinking. You sure got over being a virgin in a hell of a hurry."

"Does it bother you? That I like it so much."

"Why would it bother me?"

"I don't know."

"Put some clothes on," he said. "Got to put some food into you. Got to keep you supplied with energy."

They went to Rinaldo's and took the same booth they had shared the night before. It was twenty minutes to eleven, and the first thing she thought on noting the time was that she was late for school. She wanted to laugh. That high school would never see her again. There would be no more daydreaming at her desk, no more mindlessly writing her name in her notebook, over and over again. No more pencils, no more books —

"What's my name?"

He looked at her. "That supposed to be funny?"

"Huh?"

"As if I don't know your name? As if you don't mean anything to me?"

She put her hand on his arm. "Oh, no! That's not what I meant."

"Then what?"

"Well, you said you were registered under another name, because of the credit cards? So I thought whatever name you used, that was my name, too." She lowered her eyes. "I didn't mean for you to take it the way you thought."

She looked up hesitantly, and his face was relaxed now. The expression before had alarmed her, and the edge to his voice had very nearly made her tremble. But now everything was all right.

"Well," he said. He took out a wallet, selected a plastic card, handed it to her. "Not so loud, though."

Softly she said, "Walker P. Ferris. Who's that?"

"Oh, just an old guy."

"It's not you or anything? I mean, did you get the card under another name?"

"It's not me. Only at the motel and like that."

"Can't you get in trouble using his card?"

"Later," he said. The waitress was bringing their food. She sat in silence until the woman had set down the plates and cups of coffee and moved away. Then she said, "Can't you —"

"Get in trouble? Not hardly."

"But this Mr. Ferris, I mean the real Mr. Ferris —"

"Will the real Mr. Ferris please stand up?" He laughed shortly, easily. "Well, now, that's the point, see. The real Mr. Ferris ain't all that likely to stand up, because he was an old fellow, see, and he had an accident."

"Oh."

"What it amounts to, the real Mr. Ferris is dead. So there were his cards just going to waste, not doing him any good at all, and I thought, well, that I might have a use for them. See?"

"I guess so. It's not legal, is it?"

"Using his cards? Not exactly."

"Oh."

"That bother you?"

"Just that I don't want you to get into trouble."

"Now that's something for you not to worry about, girl. I'm not the sort to get into trouble."

She smiled back at him, then turned her

attention to the food. She had ordered the special country breakfast, eggs and country sausage and home fries and grits, plus a big glass of orange juice and a cup of coffee. It was a big breakfast and she had the appetite to do it justice. She was not usually this hungry in the morning. She wondered if the lovemaking had had something to do with it. It seemed possible. Or perhaps her hunger was more attributable to the fact that she was eating breakfast hours later than she usually did. Or to the fact that she was sitting at a table with a person she loved and not two people she hated.

Did it bother her about the credit cards? She guessed that it didn't. A man had died and Jimmie John had had the luck to make off with his wallet. Well, that wasn't going to hurt anyone, as far as she could tell. The credit card company would just get stuck for whatever he bought with the cards, seeing as Mr. Ferris wasn't alive to pay his bills. She knew that those companies were huge corporations, and a few dollars spread over everything they had wouldn't amount to much.

Anyway, it wasn't her place to be bothered or not to be bothered. He was the one using the cards, and he was the kind of person who knew what he was doing. And he cared about her, he really did. The way he'd reacted when he thought she thought he *didn't* care about her! All the warmth going out of his eyes, all the cold steel coming into his voice. He cared about her, and not just for a couple of hours, not just for a night. He really wanted her.

"Back in a minute," he said. She watched him walk to the rest rooms in back, then turned her attention to the food on her plate.

He had ordered only toast and coffee and had barely touched his toast. She raised this point when he returned.

"No appetite," he said. "Don't worry about it. I'm not much at eating on an empty stomach."

"That's why you get sick first thing in the morning. You don't eat enough."

"Oh, I get by."

"It's being alone so much and traveling all the time. You don't eat the right foods. And eating in diners all the time, it's not the same."

"I guess I don't pay much mind to what I eat."

"I wish —"

"What?"

"That we were someplace where I could

cook for you. Don't laugh, but I'm a good cook. I don't know how to cook that many things but when I make something for myself it always tastes better than my mother's cooking. And if I had cookbooks I could make just about anything you might want. It's just a question of following the directions."

"If that's all it is, you'd be surprised the number of people who can't follow directions. Some of the places I've been. It's the grease I can't take."

"You shouldn't eat greasy food. It's bad for you, and especially when you've got a sensitive stomach."

"I don't know as there's anything wrong with my stomach, exactly."

"Just that it's sensitive."

He smiled. "Well, one of these days you'll cook me a meal or two," he said, "and get my sensitive old stomach back in proper shape."

"You're just joking but I mean it."

"I know you do."

In the car she said, "I wonder what my parents are thinking right now. Be home at three thirty, blah blah blah, and then I didn't come home at all."

"I was thinking about that."

"They probably think I'm at Carolyn's house. And trying to get the phone number."

"Who's Carolyn?"

"Carolyn Fischer. She lives at Newgate Avenue near the viaduct and her father works at the B & C. The granary. And she has a little brother named Billie and her mother used to teach school before she got married. And some other things about her I don't remember. I made up a whole lot of things about Carolyn Fischer. I even made up Carolyn Fischer. There is no Carolyn Fischer."

Giggling, she told him how she had invented Carolyn as a way to avoid coming home from school. "And then she'll say, 'How come you always study at Carolyn's and never bring Carolyn over here? Are you *ashamed* of where you live?' And all the time I'm wanting to say, 'Yes, I'm *ashamed* of where I live, and *ashamed* of you and *ashamed* of my father and *ashamed* of Granny,' but instead I always keep a straight face and —"

"Wait a minute," he said. "So they'll probably try to call this Carolyn, and they won't be able to, and then what? You see what I'm getting at?"

"No."

"Next thing is they'll call the police and report you missing."

"They wouldn't do that."

"Sure they will."

"They always say I'm going to run off like Judy. Well, that's what I'm doing, aren't I? So it shouldn't be any big deal of a surprise to them."

But he was shaking his head. "They won't *know* you ran off, Betty. They'll think maybe you were in an accident, or I don't know what, and they'll call the police. Then they file a missing persons' report on you and your description goes out and everything. That means if you're just having a cup of coffee somewhere and some smartass cop recognizes you from your description, we're all in a lot of trouble."

"How would we be in trouble?"

"How old are you?"

"Sixteen in July. Why?"

"Fifteen years old. Jesus Christ."

"How old did you think I was?"

"I don't guess I thought much about it. But even if you were seventeen they could make you go back."

"They couldn't do that!"

"The hell they couldn't."

"I'd just run away again."

"And they'd just bring you back again. Even put you in a home if they felt like it. Like a prison. And while they were at it they would lock me up for running off with you."

She looked at him, eyes wide. "I never thought of that."

"I should of thought of it myself before now. Let me think a minute. All right. What we've got to do is hope they didn't call the cops already. They probably wouldn't, not the first night. They might check the hospitals to make sure you weren't in an accident but they wouldn't likely go further than that. So what we do is find a telephone and you're going to have to call them."

"I don't want to talk to them. I don't —"

"Just listen to me. Is there a time they'll both be home? A time when everybody will be home?"

"Around dinner time, probably. They're usually both home every night."

"And your grandmother too?"

"She never goes anywhere, but why —"

"You'll call them now. Whoever answers the phone, you tell them you'll be home for dinner tonight and you'll tell them everything then. You'll say you don't have time to explain anything now but you'll explain everything at dinner. Just keep talking right on through so they don't have time to interrupt and then hang up the phone."

"But I don't *want* to go there for dinner. I —"

He took hold of her wrist. "Now use your brain, Betty. Call them now and they won't be calling any police until they see you. And then we'll see them together and get your stuff and tell them we're going away together."

"They won't let us."

"Nobody stops me doing what I want to do."

"My father has a temper. You don't know what he's like."

"There'll be a phone at that drugstore. Now let's go over what you're going to say, all right?"

"All right."

"My mother was home," she said.

"What did you tell her?"

"Just like you said. I'll be home for dinner and explain everything, blah blah blah. She yelled at me."

"Hey, you're shaking, baby."

"I'm all right. She yelled at me. Not worried about was I hurt, not wanting to know how I was, just yelling that my father was mad and who did I think I was and —"

"Easy."

"That bitch."

"Don't worry about her."

"I'm all right now. Everything's all right when I'm with you. I don't want to go back there, Jimmie John."

"It's something has to be done."

"They'll make trouble."

"They won't make no trouble. And you'll need your clothes and anything else you want. They're your clothes, I guess you got a right to them."

"I can't go there alone."

"I'll be with you, baby. Right next to you."

"Okay."

He pulled the car away from the curb. "Now we got the whole afternoon to ourselves," he said, "and we can do anything you want to do. Anything at all."

She suggested the movie. He protested that she had seen it just the day before, but she told him that didn't make any difference, that it would still be like seeing it for the first time because she would be seeing it with him. But it might be a mistake to let him see the film, she added, because he would fall in love with Cybill Shepherd for sure. "Oh, I don't guess that's something you have to worry about," he said, and he squeezed her hand and gave her a look that made her melt.

They drove around, killing some time before the movie was due to start. They held hands and listened to the radio. The news came on after awhile, with a report that a gas station north of town had been held up just last night. The bandit or bandits had rifled the cash register, and the sole attendant, nineteen-year-old Richard Sturdevant of nearby Elbow Ridge, had been shot to death.

"Oh, that's terrible," she said, and Jimmie John agreed that it was.

All I can say is it's a terrible thing. He was a fine boy, hard-working, bright, ambitious. Finest boy I ever had working for me at the station.

I can't understand how it happened. I had told him to always cooperate with any holdup men, give them whatever they want, don't make any trouble for yourself. Get a license number or a description if you can but take care of yourself first and foremost. You oughta print that in your newspaper story. Might do somebody else some good.

It's a terrible shock to me.

God, Hon, what a day. Cops and reporters all over the damn station asking more questions than you'd ever believe. You see me on the six o'clock news? Somebody said they saw it, somebody drove in special to tell me about it. We'll just see if they don't run it again on the eleven o'clock.

And that kid's mother pissing and moaning all over the place. Oh, not to take away from it being a terrible thing, but I'm damned if I know what she expected out of me. You know, I'd love another beer and I don't think I've strength enough to walk into the kitchen. You sure you don't mind?

Thanks, Hon.

Now speaking good of the dead and all, but I believe I told you about that boy Dick, as to how he must have been standing in the wrong line when they handed out brains. Very day I hired him I told him last thing we want's a dead hero. Give 'em the damn money, I told him. It's all insured, let 'em take the damn money and get the hell out. The troopers'll get it back or the insurance'll pay it back and all you got to do is give 'em the money and leave well enough alone. You know how I tell that to every boy ever works for me.

All you got to do in this world is use common sense. How many times I been held up since I opened the station? Eight times, and each time I just handed over the money and that was the end of it. If I'da been there last night wouldn't of been *no trouble, not a bit of it. But this boy has to be a football hero or some such and he catches enough lead in him that it takes three men to lift him off of the floor.*

Top of the cops and reporters and what else, we must of pumped three times the gas today we normally do. Maybe four or five times, and I'd say we had ten times the number of individual sales. People would come in for a fill-up and their damn car wouldn't take more than a dollar's worth. Day shift alone I swear I took in ten times in extra sales what those sonofabitches got out of the cash register.

That is people for you. They just want to get near where the blood is. Human nature, but you think about it a little and it could make you sick.

NINE

He paid only the slightest attention to the movie. There were times when he would let himself get lost in a scene, but even then he made no attempt to relate what he was seeing to the continuity of the film, and when his attention wandered he speedily forgot what he had been watching.

Yet he enjoyed the time they spent in the quiet little movie house. The film was restful in the way that dull conversations with strangers were restful, giving his mind free rein to work its way back and forth over the problem at hand. Had the movie succeeded in absorbing his attention he would have resented it.

He liked the movie, too, for the way she got caught up in it. It amazed him that she could get that involved in something she had seen less than twenty-four hours earlier. From time to time he would turn to watch the play of emotions across her face.

Each time his gaze interrupted her concentration, and he would give her hand a light squeeze and turn his own eyes, if not his attention, back to the screen.

He let different thoughts play through his mind. It wasn't so much a question of having to figure out what to do. He already knew what he had to do. It was more a matter of fitting all the pieces into place in just the right order, and he worked this out by composing different possible scenarios and playing them out one by one. That way whatever happened he would already have given it some thought, would already have seen himself doing whatever he would have to do under certain circumstances, and there would be no danger of freezing up when push came to shove.

It was the weak ones who froze at the switch. That kid at the gas station — what was his name? He couldn't recall it at first and smiled in the darkness at the thought of it, shooting a man down one night and forgetting his name the next afternoon. He closed his eyes for a moment and put himself back to when he'd heard the name. Riding around in the car, and the radio on, and Betty sitting next to him, holding one hand while he had the other draped light and easy over the top of the wheel, and the newscaster's voice talking about the midnight robbery, and —

Richard Sturdevant. That was the name. Richard Sturdevant of nearby Elbow Bend. No, that was wrong. Elbow *Ridge.* Richard Sturdevant of nearby Elbow Ridge.

Hell, his memory wasn't so bad. His mind just had the sense to wash away those things that didn't matter. And if anything turned out to be something he wanted to remember, he could always get it back in focus. Just a matter of knowing how, knowing the tricks for getting those memories where you wanted them. Richard Sturdevant of Elbow Ridge, that was his name, all right, and now he knew it as well as the man who would soon start carving it in a chunk of granite.

When the movie ended they sat still while the credits rolled. She had the aisle seat, and without looking at him she abruptly got to her feet and began walking toward the exit. He got up immediately and followed her. Something kept him from speaking to her or taking her hand.

On the street she turned to him and with a little cry threw herself into his arms. The intensity of her embrace stunned him. Weeping openly, she kissed him again and again, clung to him.

When her passion subsided he held her at arm's length by her shoulders and looked into her eyes.

She said, "You don't understand. Yesterday I walked out of the movie still all caught up in the movie, like being a part of it. And you were there. The only good thing that ever happened to me in my life." She swallowed, wiped away tears with the back of her hand. He thought how small her wrists were; she was as fragile as a bird. "And today, I don't know how to say it. Sitting there at the end of the movie, and you know how things have a beginning and an ending, and I thought, oh, here was the movie again, and I would walk out of the theater same as yesterday, still feeling like part of the picture. And I would turn around and you would be gone. I was so *scared!* And now I can't stop crying."

He took her in his arms. He would have to buy a handkerchief, he thought. And when she wept he could blot her tears with his handkerchief.

"I know it was silly, but I couldn't get the thought to go away. A beginning and an ending —"

He took her hand. "Look," he said. He drew a circle on the back of her hand with the tip of his forefinger. "No beginning and no end," he said. "See? It just goes on, just keeps rolling along. See?"

"God, I love you."

In the car she said, "What was Mr. Ferris like?"

A dumb cocky son of a bitch, he thought. "A real sweet old boy," he said. "Kind of an old fellow, you know. A real Texas gentleman."

"How did you meet him?"

"I was hitchhiking and he picked me up."

"Hitchhiking?"

"That's right." He hesitated for a moment. "Well, see, as a matter of fact this was Mr. Ferris' car. I was hitchhiking over in Louisiana and he was on his way home to Texas and he gave me a ride. Said he normally didn't pick up hitchhikers but he was feeling poorly and had been driving all night and would be glad for someone to spell him behind the wheel."

She nodded encouragement. He was into the story now, reliving in his mind the episode he was now describing, reliving it *as* he was describing it, as if it had indeed happened that way. Such lies were effortless; they molded themselves into a subjective truth, and it was simply a matter of speaking them aloud.

Except that he did not want to lie to her. To anyone else, yes, but to her he preferred to speak truthfully. And did so whenever possible, or lied obliquely, by omission. He knew, though, that there were things she could not be allowed to know yet. When the time came she would have to know everything, but first she had to get accustomed to him, had to become a part of him as he became a part of her, and until then a certain amount of lying was inescapable.

"Now about that time I would have been pleased enough sharing the back of a pickup truck with a dozen cages of fighting cocks, which I did one time in West Florida. Getting to ride in this car, and on top of that to drive it, was just a slice of heaven for me."

"I can imagine."

"So I drove and he sat and rested hisself. First I thought he was just tired, but he didn't seem tired, talking a lot about how he made his money wildcatting for oil and all, and different stories about his life. And then he owned up that he'd been having these chest pains. Sort of like cramps in his chest, and then shooting pains up and down his left arm."

"Oh, God."

"Right. I thought just what you're thinking now, that it was his heart, and I told him I was getting off that highway and getting him to the nearest hospital in a hurry. He said no, he wanted to go home. And then he started saying that home was all he had and that was where he wanted to be if he was going to die.

"I said that was the whole point, how there was no sense in him dying if he could get to a hospital, and then he admitted to how he had two heart attacks before and either he was going to have another one now or he wasn't, and if he did, it was going to kill him as sure as hell.

"Well, just the same I took the next exit off the pike, because while he was talking he got this look of awful pain and made a sound I never hope to hear again, and I knew it was bad. I got off the highway and broke the speed laws until a cop came, and I explained what was happening and he gave me a motorcycle escort to the hospital. You want to know something? I don't even remember the name of that town the hospital was in. The whole time, like, I was in a fog."

"It must have been terrible for you."

"Worse for poor old Mr. Ferris. I guess he was still alive when we got to the hospital. But he looked like death. They took him on a stretcher and put him on one of those tables with the little wheels and rushed away with him, and then I stood around drinking coffee and waiting, and I don't know how long it was before one of the doctors came down and told me he was gone."

He drew a long breath. He could feel it all now, pacing the floor in the waiting room, then turning at the doctor's appearance and knowing without a word being spoken that the old man was dead. None of it had ever happened, but he could see and feel every fraction of it.

"So this doctor told me to have a seat; they would want to ask me some questions and get me to help them filling out a passel of forms. I was in a daze and all I knew was I wanted to be shut of that place. Gray-green walls and the smell of death all over. I went out and got in the car and just automatically started driving without knowing where I was or where I was going, just driving around and thinking.

"And then it came to me that I wasn't going back to any hospital and filling out any papers, getting myself mixed up in anything. I mean, the old man was dead and wasn't anything I could do for him. I was going to just leave the car, and then I thought, hell, why go and do that? Because Mr. Ferris had nobody, see. His wife had died a few years ago and his only son was killed in the war. 'All the money I made, boy, and I don't have anybody in the wide world.' That was how he put it. And I don't know how to explain it, but I got the feeling that it was meant for me to have the car. All his property was going to go to charities, and they would just be lumping this with everything else and auctioning it off, and I thought, well, why not use it to go where I'm going? Because the old fellow had taken a shine to me, you know. He was talking about giving me a job in his oil business. I don't know as if I would have liked that sort of work, but at the time I acted enthusiastic for fear of disappointing the man.

"I suppose you think it was wrong for me to take it."

"No."

"You don't?"

"I think he would be glad for you to have it."

He thought it over, then nodded. "Of course I won't be able to keep it forever," he said. "I knew that from the start. Legally it ain't mine, and if I was to get in any kind of trouble, say a speeding ticket or anything —"

"I didn't think of that."

"So sooner or later I'll have to put the car in a parking lot somewheres and mail the ticket and the keys back to the state of Texas. All I have is the use of it. Are you crying again?"

"No. I was just thinking about that poor old man."

"Well, you know, everybody dies."

"I know it."

"And he had a good life."

"But not having anybody at the end. His wife and his son dead, and not having anybody."

"I never had anybody either. Until now."

He pulled to the curb. "They'll have a pay phone inside," he said. "Here's a dime. You call home and make sure your mother and father are both there."

"She said they would be. When I called before —"

"Let's make sure. No use talking to one of them and not the other. Suppose we got it all straight with your mother, and then your father came home and wouldn't listen to a word she said, but went on and put the cops on us? And you fifteen years of age and me with a car that don't legally belong to me, and then where in the hell would we be?"

"Okay."

"All you got to do is make sure the two of them are home. Then we'll drive over there and have it out with them once and for all, and you'll grab your clothes and whatever else you want to take —"

"I can have everything packed in ten minutes."

"Say five minutes to get over there and fifteen minutes to talk some sense into them and ten minutes to pack. Five and fifteen is twenty and ten is thirty minutes and we'll be on our way out of this town and never have to look at it again."

"You say fifteen minutes to talk some sense into them. I never did it in fifteen *years*."

"Go make that call now."

When she entered the store he unlocked the glove compartment and took out the gun. It still held one bullet. He loaded it with four more, leaving the chamber under the hammer empty. You had to take chances, but you didn't have to chance carrying a round under the hammer and maybe blowing your balls off by accident. He wedged the gun under his belt and fixed his jacket so it draped over the gun butt. He put a half dozen shells in his jacket pocket and returned the box of shells to the glove compartment and locked it again.

She came back, her face flushed with excitement. "They're both home. It was him answered the phone. My father. He just yelled at me. He didn't listen to anything I said. I almost hung up on the bastard without saying a word."

"And your mother —"

"Oh, she's there. I heard her whining in the background. I said we'd be right over."

"You were right about that."

She touched his arm. "Jimmie John? I know what you said and all, but maybe we shouldn't go. Or just I'll go and I'll get out somehow. But he's big, and I can tell he's been drinking all day, and when he loses his temper he's something fierce."

His hand itched to pat the gun butt. "It's got to be done," he told her. "And there's nothing to worry about. I can take care of myself."

He parked the car in front of the white frame house. Betty got out of the car immediately and started up the path. He had to hurry to catch up with her. He was at her side when the door opened and a man stood blocking the doorway. He wasn't all that big. Beefy like that Richard Sturdevant kid, but twice as old and soft in the gut. And you could see he'd been drinking. It showed in his eyes, and the looseness of his mouth.

To his daughter he said, "Get in here, you little tramp. Get in this house before I break your damn neck." He stepped aside, and when Betty darted past him Jimmie John was right behind her, moving quickly into the living room. Frank Deinhardt spun around and glared at him.

"Now just who in the hell do you think you are?"

Softly, now, politely. "My name is Jimmie John Hall, sir, and I —"

"You been with her, you son of a bitch?"

"Betty and I love each other, Mr. Deinhardt. We —"

"You get out of this house before I beat the living shit out of your fucking little head. You son of a bitch. Just who in the hell do you think you are, anyhow?"

He rolled with it, keeping up his part of the conversation, letting the words pad around him like mood music. His eyes took in the room, and it was as if he had been in it once before. He had not tried to picture this room earlier, but now it seemed that everything was just as he had somehow known it would be. The television set with the toothless, flatulent grandmother perched in front of it, seemingly oblivious to the hell that was breaking loose around her. The other woman, Betty's mother, standing there like some kind of idiot, wringing her hands and darting angry looks first at him, then at Betty. The framed landscape print on the wall over the sagging slip-covered davenport. The chest of drawers, the top ringed by neglected beer cans. The silk-covered pillow on the davenport: SOUVENIR OF SILVER DOLLAR CITY. A wedding picture in a dime-store frame on top of the television set.

He had never been here before. Betty had supplied no more in the way of description than to furnish the room with the television set and to prop the old woman on a chair in front of it. And yet he knew this room. He recognized it.

And now he said, "You can't stop us, Mr. Deinhardt. Betty and I are going away together. We just came back to tell you, and so that Betty could get her clothes."

"You little prick. You know how old she is?"

"She's fifteen."

"She's fifteen, damn you! You little shit, they'll throw you in jail and leave you there for twenty fucking years." He whirled toward Betty, a hand gesturing wildly. "And you, you little whore, you little piece of filth! You're worse than your sister. She was bad enough, but by God if you're not worse. She at least didn't have the nerve to let a boy get at her and then bring him into her own home."

"This is not my home. My home is with Jimmie John, wherever we are. That's my home. This was never my home."

Good girl, Betty.

"You slut," Deinhardt said, and moved to slap her.

Now.

He said, "Mr. Deinhardt —" And moved between the man and the girl, his hands up to block the blow. With a roar the older man swung at him, but before the blow could land Jimmie John was already falling back, going with the punch. The heavy fist grazed his jaw but he did not even feel it.

But no one could have known this. Because he went on falling, as if recoiling from a terrible clout, stumbling backwards

184

and sprawling over a footstool and onto the floor. The footstool was one added touch of realism he could have done without. He had not known it was there. He landed a little harder than he had expected, and decided it was probably a very good idea there wasn't a round under the hammer of the revolver.

His eyes took in everything as if the moment were frozen. Deinhardt standing there, glaring. Betty's mother at her husband's side, mouth open like a fish, eyes registering a mixture of shock and hatred. And Betty herself, stunned at first, then scampering to his side.

He sat up, fending her off with his left arm. "I'm all right," he told her. And he waited a beat, then took a step toward her father.

"Get out of here, you little bastard!"

"You can't make me leave, Mr. Deinhardt."

Come on, damn you.

And he waited, his mind rehearsing his hand's moves, waited while Deinhardt made up his mind. Waited while the man lowered his head and committed himself with a first step. Waited until Deinhardt, hands extended like hooks, halved the distance between them.

And then the gun was in his hand.

He even had time to aim. He was so fast and the rest of the world so slow. He snapped off a shot and the bullet took Frank Deinhardt in the groin and spilled his legs out behind him. He plunged on forward, piled onto the footstool, crashed to the floor at Jimmie John's feet.

Betty, I just shot your father's balls off. Now there's nobody you belong to but me.

He caught a glimpse of the grandmother's crazy old eyes. She was watching them now instead of the television set, but her expression was as it had been before. As if to say that the action was crisp and interesting enough, and she would as soon stay with this particular channel, at least until the next Polident commercial.

Betty's mother was keening, making a thin wild sound, like something he might have heard vaguely in the mists of a cough syrup dream. Deinhardt moaned and his feet twitched. Jimmie John walked around him, turned up the volume on the television set.

He caught sight of Betty's face but wrenched his eyes away. He could not look at her just now.

He shot Frank Deinhardt in the back of his fat neck and the twitching feet went still. He turned to Betty's mother and drank in the horror in her eyes. She had one hand to her open mouth, but she was still making that weird sound. She took small backward steps until the wall got in her way. She flattened up against the wall. Her housedress had a floral pattern and so did the wallpaper.

You can't hide that way, Mother, he thought. And wanted to laugh.

He took a step toward her and shot her in the chest. The bullet pressed her even tighter against the wall and she was a long time falling. He shot her again on the way down.

Before she hit the floor he wheeled around and headed for Granny. She didn't try to move and her face showed no change in expression. She farted noisily and laughter bubbled hysterically in his chest but stayed inside. He put the muzzle of the gun to the old woman's temple and blew her brains out.

That emptied the gun. He took three shells from his jacket pocket and loaded three chambers. He gave them each one more round in the head.

Everything was spinning. He took deep breaths and held them in and made the spinning stop.

He looked at Betty. Her mouth was moving but he couldn't hear her over the television set and didn't know whether she was talking or merely mouthing words. He dug a shell out of his pocket and stuffed it into a chamber, and he caught a look of terror in Betty's eyes, but of course the bullet was not for her, how could she possibly think it was for her, and he spun around and shot the television set. The picture tube exploded with a noise greater than the gunshot. Glass clattered for long seconds, and then the room was as silent as death.

She said, "Oh God, oh God. They're all dead. You killed them all, they're all dead, you killed them all."

He moved toward her. *Don't draw away from me,* he told her silently. *Please, please, don't draw away from me.*

She very nearly did. He saw her muscles tighten and thought she was about to take a step backward, but then the tension fell away and her shoulders dropped an inch and he knew it was all right.

She was his now. And he had to have her now. Now, right away, this minute.

He advanced on her, tearing his own clothes off with one hand, shrugging out of

188

the jacket, opening the pants and stepping out of them. His other hand still gripped the gun. He got hold of her and drew her moaning down to the carpet. He pulled up her skirt and got her panties down and took her.

Took her just like that. Fiercely, without preliminaries, on the floor of her parents' living room in the center of a triangle of corpses. Her father and her mother and her grandmother lay dead around them and the gun that had killed them was clutched tight in his right hand, its hot barrel inches from her cheek, and he hammered at her with measured powerful strokes, pounded against her ridge of pubic bone, buried himself again and again in her flesh.

At first she was simply present. Then she began to respond, and he felt her fighting her own response, resisting it. But she could not resist it, and soon she was no longer trying to resist but was moving with him, and he was completely in control, perfectly in control, able to last forever if he had to, and her fingernails were in his shoulders and she was crying and moaning and yes, now, now —

First for her. Because he could not possibly get off until she did, it was all for her now, and then it happened for her and she went with it, embraced all of it, and then he could will the mechanism that was holding him back, could permit it to let go, and he stroked twice more, in and out the sweet length of her, and erupted.

And Richard Sturdevant of nearby Elbow Ridge was standing there with sweat pouring off his fat face, hands out in front of him to catch bullets in midair, but instead he caught one in the belly and one in the chest and one in the middle of his forehead. He missed one, let it get away from him and bounce off the ceiling, but he caught three out of four and that wasn't a bad average for a kid his age.

Bodies pressed together and his heart hammering and his whole body so alive, so alive.

And Walker P. Ferris was stretched out on his back in a Texas cow pasture, stark naked and unconscious from a blow on the head, and a piece of pipe went up and came down and went up and came down and went up and came down, and Walker P. Ferris was stretched out on his back in a Texas cow pasture, stark naked and dead from a blow on the head.

Her head was turned to the side, toward the revolver that he still held tightly in his hand. She might have been staring at it but her eyes were shut.

And her father, roaring like a bull, charging like a bull, until a matador timed the thrust just right and the bull fell like a ton of dead meat at the matador's feet. And her mother spread out against the wall like a butterfly spread on a mounting board, and pinned in place with a bullet. And her grandmother, watching live television until the picture tube blew out and took her head along with it.

He took more deep breaths and let everything slide back into place. He eased his weight off of her and stretched out at her side. They did not have time to waste. Still, he could let her sleep for a minute or two. He loved the look of her face when she slept. And it was amazing to him the way her passion took her immediately into unconsciousness. He had heard of such things but had never believed they actually happened.

He put out a hand and stroked her cheek and throat. He flashed the rabbit that had hurled itself against his car, the rabbit he had held in his hands before covering it over with grass. But the rabbit he flashed was alive, lying gentle and secure in his hands, trusting his hands, little heart fluttering under soft fur, long ears laid back, little nose twitching, safe and warm and alive in his hands.

He moved to kiss her face. "Okay, little girl," he said. "Time to wake up. C'mon, baby. We got places to go."

She opened her eyes and blinked at him. She started to cry, but he held her and stroked her hair and she stopped crying and was all right.

"A terrible, terrible tragedy."

"They were a fine upstanding family. They were Christians. When something like that happens to ordinary people you wonder what kind of a world we're living in."

"I'm sure that little girl will never be seen alive. They'll find her lying dead in a ditch. I can't bear to think what she'll have gone through first."

"Whoever did it should be shot down like a dog."

"I keep a gun in my house. Always have. My wife doesn't like the sight of it. Doesn't care for guns. Well, she is going to get used to the sight of it, and the touch of it, and the sound of it. By God, starting

tonight she is going to learn how to use it."

"I don't guess I'll sleep proper till they get the man who did this."

"You work hard all your life and somebody comes and takes it all away from you."

"Must have sold twenty guns the first hour this morning. And ammunition, I can't keep it in stock."

"Hanging's too good for him."

"When a nation turns its back on God —"

"Hanging's too good for him."

"Animals."

"Hanging's too good for him."

"Hanging's too good for him."

"Hanging's too good for him."

TEN

The cabin was small and primitive. There was room for the double bed and the chest of drawers and not much more. The bathroom was in the same category of contradictions as green blackboards and plastic glasses. You couldn't bathe in it. There was no tub, no shower, only a washbowl and a toilet. Drips from the two faucets had worn iron-red channels in the porcelain of the sink. There was no door to the bathroom, incredibly enough, and she kept having to use the toilet. She didn't like doing this, not with him stretched out on the bed just a few yards away, but her bowels gave her no choice. She knew how fastidious he was and hoped he would not lose respect for her.

But he seemed completely oblivious. He was stretched out on his back with his eyes closed. He had taken off his clothes and the bedsheet covered him almost to the neck. His hands were outside of the sheet.

She found herself frequently looking at his hands and arms, and it was as if they were disembodied, lying there on either side of a white cotton mound with which they had no real connection.

The cabin was one of a dozen just beyond Thedford, about a hundred and forty miles northwest of Grand Island. It had taken them two and a half hours to cover the distance, and she could barely remember the ride. There had been little in it to remember. He drove while she sat beside him. Neither of them talked much.

The interval between their violent love-making and the drive was blurred in her recollection in another way. She remembered the details well enough — going upstairs, putting things into a suitcase, pausing to comb her hair and wash her hands and face. Returning reluctantly to the first floor and trying to walk through the living room without looking at the bodies, but being unable to avoid staring at each in turn. She remembered all of this, and yet somehow there was a haze around her memory like thin clouds around the moon. Perhaps it was that she herself had been in a daze during that time, moving around and performing tasks but not really entirely there.

When she was ten a teacher had pushed a door open suddenly while she was walking past it, and the heavy oak had struck her with force in the temple. She was taken immediately to the school nurse, who had her lie down for a few moments, gave her the inevitable aspirin, peered curiously into her eyes and nose and ears, made her gag on a wooden tongue depressor, and at last pronounced her fit as a fiddle and sent her back to class. She remained in school that day until the final bell, participating in class exactly as she had always done. When school let out she walked home, had a glass of milk and a cookie, and went to her room to lie down. She slept for four hours, and when she awoke she was perfectly all right, the same as ever, but the memory of that interval between sustaining the concussion and going to bed was blurred much as this present memory was. As though she had not been entirely herself during that particular period of time.

She sat on the edge of the bed now and looked at him. A few hours ago he had killed her father and her mother and her grandmother while she watched with — what? She did not even know. And now she looked at him and knew that she was in love with him and did not know what it all meant.

She had hated her father. And her mother. And if she had not hated Granny, she had certainly felt nothing but contempt for the woman, and had frequently thought that she would be better off dead than alive. Well, she was dead now. They were all dead, the three of them.

He did things with such instant assurance. He never hesitated. He had been very decent with her father, had spoken so softly and politely, and then when her father hit him and was going to kill him, then all at once there was a gun in his hand and before she really knew what was happening all three of them were dead. He would just act, suddenly and surely, and things began and ended in a flash.

And then afterward, while the three of them lay there —

She made her mind skip that part for now. She thought instead about the end of the ride, the sudden screech of brakes, the way she heaved against her seat belt as he spun the car to the left and onto the cinder driveway that led to the tourist cabins. "We're stopping here. I can't drive any more tonight. I have to crash."

"It looks sort of rundown," she had offered. "Do you want to wait and try the next place down the road? It might not be very nice here."

"We'll stay here."

"All right."

"I'll go and register. You get down so they can't see you, see? You're the one they'll be looking for."

"Do you think —"

"Not yet, but sooner or later, and then they'll be showing your picture around. And somebody might remember seeing you. Nobody knows to look for me."

He had parked the car in shadows, left her there while he went into the office unit. She waited nervously for him and thought about what he had said. They would be looking for her. They had stopped at her house to talk her parents out of calling the police, so that they would not have to worry about people looking for her, and now her parents and grandmother were dead and they would be searching for someone far more important to them than a teenage runaway.

But what could he have done? Her father was going to beat him up, possibly beat him to death knowing the man's temper and his physical strength. He could only defend himself with the gun, and —

She had never known he had a gun. Actually there was not much she did know about him. And yet she knew him, and he knew her, in ways no one had ever known either of them before. She was sure of this.

In their cabin he had gritted his teeth at the appearance of the place, then cursed quietly but thoroughly at the lack of a shower. He sponged himself at the sink, shaved, brushed his teeth. Then drank some cough medicine and took a red pill and stretched out on the bed.

She thought about going to sleep herself and knew it was impossible. She was exhausted, drained, and yet she had never been more intensely awake in her life. One of those little red pills of his might let her rest, but she didn't like the idea of taking one. There were kids in school who took pills, uppers and downers and things she didn't know the name of. There were kids who smoked grass, and there was talk that some of the seniors took acid trips. But she had never taken anything stronger than the coffee her father had forbidden her.

It was hard for her to sit still but the cabin offered no room to pace the floor. She went to the bathroom and washed her hands and face again. There was an unframed square mirror a foot square over the washbowl. She looked into it and tried to read something in the face reflected there. She felt that she should be altered in some way by what she had experienced, but her face looked as it had always looked to her.

There was no television set, but on top of the chest of drawers was an old radio. You had to put a quarter in it for a half hour's listening.

She went over to the bed and said, "Would it be all right if I played the radio?"

He didn't answer, and she decided not to risk waking him. She sat down again and had gone on to think of something else when he said, "Go ahead and play it. It won't bother me."

"I thought you were asleep."

"Not asleep and not awake. Go ahead."

His change was on top of the dresser. She took a quarter and put it in the slot. She turned the volume down low so that it wouldn't keep him awake.

The radio helped her avoid thinking. She listened to it without paying it much attention. Sometimes she would turn to look at him. He never changed position, lay absolutely motionless. She listened to Tammy Wynette and Buck Owens and Waylon

Jennings and Jeannie C. Riley. When the ten o'clock news came on she heard about a Congressional investigation into meat prices and a snag in disarmament talks, and she wasn't paying much attention to any of this, and then the voice was saying

"— breakthrough in the investigation of last night's robbery homicide in Grand Island. State Police sources reported tonight that a crumpled sales slip has given them a strong lead to the vehicle used in the gas station holdup in which nineteen-year-old Richard Sturdevant lost his life. The slip was one which young Sturdevant made out incorrectly, and a check revealed that a correct slip for that particular sale was not to be found.

"A call to Standard's credit card department established the card as the property of a Mr. Walker P. Ferris of Balch Springs, Texas. Ferris, a Texas businessman, was expected home several days ago. His wife told investigators she has not heard from him in almost a week, but that his business ventures require considerable travel and that she was not unduly alarmed by his extended absence.

"Ferris was driving a new Oldsmobile Toronado, blue with a white top. The car bears Texas license plates. The license

*number is 4-YJ-302. Let me repeat that —
4-YJ — that's Y as in Young J as in
John — 302. Police at the present have
expressed no opinion as to whether Ferris
is a suspect in the robbery and murder or
whether he himself may have been an
earlier victim of an as yet unknown killer.
A special police number has been established to take calls from anyone having information on the Ferris automobile. The
number to call is —"*

He gave the number and repeated the
description of the car. She waited for him
to say more, and then he was talking about
a tanker truck carrying a load of propane
gas which had overturned near Flagstaff,
Arizona, and she got up and turned off the
radio.

It couldn't be. It was all wrong. He must
have bought gas there that afternoon and
the sales slip got lost or something. The
robbery had taken place late last night and
he was with her that night, she remembered when she first heard about it, remembered thinking how it must have
happened just while they were making
love. He was with her, he couldn't have
been at that gas station and —

But he had gone out. He left her to sleep
and went out for a little while. For how

long? Not long enough to rob a gas station, certainly. Not long enough to kill someone.

He did things so quickly. Made up his mind and did them and they were over. How long had he been gone? She had been asleep, she didn't know. But all at once he was back and he was making love to her and —

He had made love to her tonight, too. On her living room floor, with the barrel of his gun still hot.

No. No, this was all impossible. Talking about Walker P. Ferris' wife, and how she was expecting him to come home, but Walker P. Ferris had died in a hospital and his wife had died years and years ago, that was what was so sad, the rich old man who had no one in the world, and that was why Jimmie John had known it was only right to take the car and —

"Jimmie John!"

He didn't move. She put her hand on his bare shoulder under the sheet. Her fingertips felt the bone close beneath the skin. She shook him and said his name again, and his eyes opened and locked with hers.

"They know about the car!"

"What are you talking about?"

"On the radio. They know about the car;

they gave a description and the license plate number and everything. They —"

"That's impossible. Nobody saw us."

"There was a credit card slip. At the Standard station."

He sat up. His eyes were so sharp she felt impaled upon them. He said, "When was this?"

"Just now. On the ten o'clock news. What are we going to do?"

"Tell me everything you heard."

"They know about the car. They know about Mr. Ferris, but they think maybe he was the killer. They —"

"Slow down and back up. Steady down, Betty. Everything is gonna stay nice and cool. Just go back to the beginning and tell me everything they said."

She couldn't tell it in order. She had to back up and fill in a couple of times, and when she had finished he took her back over it and questioned her on a couple of points, his voice as calm and level as if he were inquiring about a weather forecast. When he was satisfied he got out of bed and began dressing.

She said, "What are we going to do?"

"We're going to get the hell out of here. Soon as the sky lights up some son of a bitch'll see that car and they'll throw the whole National Guard around this cabin. I got to get us a car."

"How?"

"There's other people staying here. All I got to do is get somebody's keys and we got us a car."

"But —"

"First step is to move this one around in back so nobody sees it from the road. You stay right here. I'll be a couple of minutes. You stay right inside here and wait and I won't be more than a couple of minutes."

There were so many things she had to ask him. But he didn't give her time to put her thoughts together. He went out the door and closed it behind him and she looked at the closed door and wanted to scream. But she did not scream.

She was still looking at the door when it opened. Her mind was wandering and it startled her when the door burst open. Her first reaction was that it was *Them.*

But it was Jimmie John. He had a ring of keys in his hand and he was grinning.

The new car was a two-year-old Dodge station wagon. There were candy wrappers on the floor and cigarette butts in the ashtray. The windshield on her side had a streak from a defective wiper blade.

They were heading south now. They had backtracked to Thedford and headed south on 83. "They'll find the car and figure we kept on in the same direction," he explained. "We were going northwest. So now we back up a few miles and cut south while they're running around looking for us in Wyoming or some such place."

"They'll know to look for this car, won't they?"

"Not just yet they won't. I don't figure to keep this car forever." He patted her hand. "Tell the truth, I'm not all that fond of it. That Toronado was a beautiful car. Knew all along I couldn't keep it forever, but I sure wanted to."

"I couldn't believe it about the gas station."

"Oh."

"I just couldn't believe it."

He drove awhile in silence. Then he said, "It was him or me, Betty. Came at me with a tire iron. Damn fool to charge a gun with a tire iron, and nothing I could do but put a bullet in him. It was that or stand there and let him split my head."

"Like with my father, hitting you and coming at you the way he did."

"Like that."

She hesitated, then nodded. "I guess it must of been while I was sleeping. At the motel."

"That's right. I had to get us some money, you know. Knew I couldn't use the credit cards much longer." He laughed shortly. "Used 'em one more time than I shoulda done."

"Jimmie John? Whose car is this? That we're in now?"

"You can say it's ours now."

"I mean who did you take it from?"

He glanced at her, then turned his eyes back to the road. Suddenly he laughed. He said, "Never saw anything like it in my life. You might of noticed there were two cars there besides ours. So after I moved the Toronado I checked 'em both out, because sometimes people'll leave keys in the ignition. Be surprised how many people will do that. Not this time. So I took a look at the two cabins, and one's got the lights on and the other doesn't, and I figured the hell with trying to wake some fool up and I went to the lit one.

"Never even locked the door. I had my foot back to kick it in and then I thought, hell, try the knob first, and I turned it and walked right in. And there they are, going at it a mile a minute. Man and a woman, both of 'em naked as jaybirds, and he's this little guy with these little wire-rim glasses stuck up on his nose so he won't miss seeing a thing, and she's forty years old trying to look seventeen, makeup and lipstick and all, and I won't tell you what they were doing."

She did not want to ask but couldn't help herself. "Never you mind," he said. "Just say it was nothing to be proud of. And they looked up, you know, first him and then her, and they didn't know whether to shit or go blind. I said to give me the car keys or I'd blow his damn head off, and he just said, 'On the dresser, on the dresser, and take the money too.' Like it wouldn't occur to me to take the money without his damn permission."

"You shot them."

"I figured you probably heard the shots."

"No. Or I did and didn't know it." She was just so tired and everything was pressing down on her. "I just . . . I don't know. I just knew you shot them. My father and my mother and my grandmother and that boy at the gas station and now these people. What were their names?"

"I don't know. I left the wallet; I just took the money out. Maybe there's something in the glove compartment with their

209

names on it. His name, I mean. She ain't his wife, you can bet on that. You don't do things like that with your wife."

"I don't want to know their names."

"Whatever you say."

"But I'll hear them anyway. On the radio. Tomorrow, the next day."

"I had to do it, Betty." His voice was different now. The lightness was gone. "If I left them alive they'd be on the phone to the police five minutes after we left. And they'd give them a description of the car and the license number and we'd be right back where we were, with a car that's getting talked about on every police radio around."

"They'll know about the car anyway. When they find the bodies."

That's not until morning. Because nobody'll go into the cabin until nine o'clock at the earliest, and that gives us all those hours in the meantime to put all the miles we can between us and them. I had to buy us that time. Don't you see?"

She saw. She kept seeing things and not wanting to see them. The gas station attendant and her father and her mother and her grandmother and the man and the woman. Six people. And who else? Walker P. Ferris? Probably. If Walker P. Ferris had a wife, after everything he'd said about the man being a widower, maybe that whole story about the heart attack and the breakneck trip to the hospital was equally false. But the way he had talked about it, the way he made the man come alive for her as he spoke —

After awhile she asked where they were going. South, he said. South and west. Colorado, New Mexico. Someplace where they would be safe.

She said, "Safe?"

He looked at her.

"In the morning they'll find the man and the woman," she said. "And they'll know about this car, so we'll have to get another one, and then another one after that, and then —"

He stomped on the brake pedal. She was hurled forward against her seat belt. He pulled off the road and put the transmission in Park and turned toward her, and she thought he was going to kill her.

He said, "Now listen to me. Will you listen to me? There's dead bodies all over this state now, six of them. That is murder. It is not stealing nickels out of a parking meter. That means if they get me I die. Do you understand that? *I die*."

She saw him dead then, and for an instant her veins ran ice water. The image was unbearable. Her family, the gas station attendant, the man and woman — she could somehow stand these images, these images of reality, but the fantasy image of Jimmie John dead was unacceptable.

"I have to get us away," he said. "And that means doing what I have to do. Whatever it is. That man and woman bought us maybe ten hours. Damn it, do you know what kind of people they were? For you to be crying over them?"

"I wasn't —"

"She had his *pecker* in her *mouth,* god damn it! She was *sucking* his *cock!*" He closed his eyes for a moment. Softly, as if to himself, he said, "The thing is that you don't see what's happening. All my life moving around, here and there and everywhere, and never getting anyplace at all, never adding up to anything, never being anybody, and all of a sudden everything starts coming together." He made a fist of his hand and thumped the steering wheel. "Everything coming together for me, and I would know about everything in advance, I would see it coming, and I would just do everything just right, smooth as silk, everything neat and clean and razor-sharp. First the car and then you, everything good happening to me right on schedule, just *knowing* to wait for the right car, just *knowing* to stay in Grand Island and drive around until I found the right girl, and searching all my life for the right girl and then missing you coming out of school, never seeing you, and then getting another chance with you walking out of the movie just as I'm driving past it, and one look at you and one look from you and that was it. Remember?"

She nodded.

"Every single thing just right. Remember asking me what your name was, and me taking it the wrong way? I thought you thought I didn't actually remember your name. Shit, I knew every damn thing about you just looking at you. I knew more about you then in that minute than you ever knew about yourself.

"And now everything's coming together faster and faster, and I'm still on top of it, I know I am, and it's going to work out. Because it's all written down somewhere. It's all planned, and I'm keyed into it right now and all the speed and power is flowing right through me. Do you understand what I'm saying?"

"I think so."

He took her chin between his thumb and

forefinger. He said, "You maybe think that I'm crazy."

"No."

"Maybe you do. The things I'm saying, they *sound* crazy, don't they?"

"I don't know."

"They do. Don't think I don't know it. If I heard somebody else talking like this I'd figure he was crazy. My mother had me in a home for a couple years and there was one kid there and he was crazy. He counted his steps. He'd be walking around. 'Ninety-seven, ninety-eight, ninety-nine, hundred, hundred and one, hundred and two,' just counting every time he picked his foot up and set it down, and he'd lose count and start over a dozen times a day. The goddamnedest thing you ever saw, never taking a step without counting it." He frowned. "The older boys used to do things with him. You know what I'm talking about?"

"I'm not sure."

"I mean like sex things."

"That's what I thought."

"He would do anything, see. I never did anything like that. Never. It's the truth."

"I believe you."

"I never wanted to lie to you. God *damn* it. I told you some lies that I can't tell you

214

the truth of them yet. But I will. You got to give me time."

"All right."

"Twenty-two years I never told anybody anything. Hard to turn it all around in a day."

"I understand."

"Betty? You can get out of this, you know. I can let you out of the car and you walk to some farmhouse and holler for the cops. Tell 'em you were a hostage, I held a gun on you and made you come with me. Killed your parents, killed the man and the woman, and you didn't have a chance to get loose until now. Then at least you're shut of it."

"No."

"Have to do it now, though. Much longer and it'd be hard for them to buy it. You want to do that? Just get out of the car and start walking. Give me a little time to get out of the area, that's all. And don't give 'em my name. You want to do that, baby?"

"No. Don't make me go."

"Make you? I'd of near died if you wanted to. But I'd of let you."

"I just want to be with you."

He took her hand and squeezed it, hard. She drew a deep breath and closed her eyes.

She said, "I just —"

"What?"

"Killing people. Will you have to . . . do it again?"

"Not once we're out of this."

"But until then —"

"Maybe yes, maybe no."

"I just hate that, Jimmie John."

" 'Course you do."

"I *do!*"

His eyes challenged her. He said, "I seem to remember a certain person lyin' back on a livin' room floor and not hatin' one solitary minute of it."

"That wasn't because of the killing."

"Wasn't it?"

"No!"

He frowned for a moment. "You wearing panties under that skirt?"

"Why?"

"Are you? Take 'em off."

"What for?"

"Just take 'em off. Now come on over here." He put his right arm around her shoulders and his left hand on her knee. His hand moved up along her thigh. She parted her legs for him and he touched her.

"Now I'm gonna tell you something. I told you about that man and that woman.

Little guy with funny glasses, big fat-butted woman with black hair and makeup and big floppy titties, and she's all curled up at the foot of the bed sucking on him while he's got his head propped on a pillow and his glasses on so's he can watch. Well, I got the car keys, and I got the money from his wallet, and he's all shaking and her eyes are rolling all over her head.

"So I make her do it again. What she was doing when I came on into the cabin. Told her if she didn't do it I was goin' to kill her. And she didn't want to, see, but I stuck that old gun in her face and said it was suck that or the other and she could decide which.

"So she did it. I just watched her for a minute or so, and wanted to throw up but controlled it, you can control those things when you have to, and I watched her for maybe a minute and then I shot her in the back of the neck and him in the chest. And I left them like that, see, with his pecker still in her mouth. That's how I left them.

"And I liked doing it. I better tell you that. I liked doing it. Just the way you like hearing about it, because look what it's doing to you, look how hot you are. Aren't you? Aren't you?"

His fingers stroked her and she wanted

to scream but didn't scream, wanted to draw away but didn't draw away, wanted to turn lifeless and numb but didn't. She could not resist him. All he had to do was put a hand on her and her capacity for resistance vanished. Her own passion disgusted her, but her disgust could not cool it by a degree.

Just his fingers. Just his hand beneath her skirt. Until at last she sobbed and trembled and sagged against him, spent, complete.

The car was moving. She was back on her own side of the car, her seat belt again fastened around her middle. Evidently her orgasm had put her to sleep again. It was embarrassing the way that happened.

She said, "You can do anything you want with me. You know that, don't you?"

"You ought to get some sleep, baby. You want to get in back? I'll put the back seat down and you can stretch out and get comfortable."

"I want to stay up front with you."

"Close your eyes, then. It's getting late."

"What about you?"

"Well, I guess I better stay awake, being as I'm the one doing the driving."

"You must be exhausted."

"I'm all right."

"But you were tired before, and then you didn't get any sleep."

"I took a pill."

"I thought that was to help you sleep."

"There's others to keep you on top of things. And awake. I took some before."

"Pills to wake up and pills to go to bed."

"Yeah. Ain't science grand?"

"Maybe we'll open a drugstore," she said. Her eyes were closed now and she had trouble getting words together. "In Mexico," she said. "Just the two of us."

She felt his hand on hers, and then everything clouded over and she slept.

It is on my mind all the time. I scarcely think of anything else, and most nights I will dream on it. I will dream it just the way it happened, except that it will be stretched out in time the way things are in dreams. The trigger of my police-special will take me forever to pull, and the bullet that hit me, in my dreams it is as if I see it coming all the way just floating at me in slow motion, and I just cannot move to get out of the way of it.

Thinking on it when I am awake, now, I keep trying to find ways to make it come out different than it did. Like dropping to the ground and firing out of a prone position, so as to present less of a target area and get more stability in aiming and shooting. Prone is best and kneeling is second-best and standing is worst of all. I was taught this as a rookie cop and always knew it but when things pop sudden there is so little time. You have no time for thinking but must act right off the top of yourself. Then you have the rest of your life to think how you should have done it.

In dreams, with the time element all stretched out and with knowing how it comes out while it is happening, that has got to be the worst. All of this shooting and missing, shooting and missing, shooting and missing. That is the worst thing there is, to be aiming at a man, shooting at him, and just to miss him time and time again.

ELEVEN

And I'm gonna spend the rest of my life
Not comin' home to you

While she slept, he kept the car radio tuned to KOMA, a clear-channel station out of Omaha. Commercial sponsorship thinned out in the late hours, and the disc jockey would play three or four records in a row without interrupting for a commercial. Every half hour there was a five-minute news summary. He kept hearing the same items over and over — an investigation of meat prices, a four-car collision on Route 64 outside of Council Bluffs, Iowa, a wrecked truck that spilled a load of propane somewhere in Arizona.

And, with slight changes from time to time, the story of what had happened in Grand Island.

The first two newscasts mentioned nothing about the gas station holdup, nothing of the massacre at the Deinhardt house. At midnight he was on Route 30 heading west from North Platte, rolling toward the Colorado line, and the first break came.

The details were skimpy, the facts not entirely accurate. The family name of the victims was given as Reinhart and the number of corpses reported as four. The bodies had been discovered when a neighbor got curious about why all the lights in the house were on so late. She went over, knocked, opened the door, and walked in on the death scene. State and local police investigators were on the scene, and a break in the case was expected shortly.

Sure it was, he thought. If they couldn't even count dead bodies, how could they expect to get anywhere?

He checked the gas gauge. Just a gallon or two left, and soon it would not be safe to stop. Or was it safe to stop now? They wouldn't be looking for him, but someone could remember the car later on and the police would know which way they had come. He slowed the car at an open station at Ogallala. There were cars at two of the pumps, and one was a police cruiser. He put his foot down on the accelerator and moved on.

Cops. There they sat, filling their car with gas and theirselves with coffee, while he drove right on by them. And they would never know it.

There was another station on the other side of town. It was closed, but he had already decided that a station closed for the night was safer. There were several cars parked in back to the left of the station itself, a little building elaborately constructed to resemble a log cabin. He pulled the wagon in line with the others, and when he turned off the ignition Betty opened her eyes.

"According to the radio," he told her, "you're dead." When she wrinkled her forehead at him he explained, "It was on the news. Said they found four bodies at your house, so unless somebody crawled in and died there for the pure hell of it, somebody made a mistake. Found out there were four in the family and added up two and two and look what they got." He leaned over and kissed her. "You look pretty healthy for a dead girl," he said.

"Don't say that."

"About looking healthy?"

"About the other. I don't want to think about it." She stretched her arms over her head. "Where are we?"

"Nowhere special. A gas station. It's closed, but I mean to open it up."

"What if there's a burglar alarm?"

"In the middle of the country?" He opened his door. "You wait here. They maybe locked the pumps, but they maybe left the key around. I'll have a look."

The pumps were locked, as he'd half-expected. People just didn't trust their fellow man nowadays. He broke a pane of glass in the door of the simulated log cabin, reached through and turned the lock. He searched carefully, but if there were any keys for the pumps he couldn't find them. On a board near the door there were a few sets of car keys. He guessed they probably belonged to the other cars parked outside and thought of switching vehicles. It stood to reason, though, that those cars had been brought in for repair, and there was every likelihood that they hadn't been worked on yet. With his luck he would pick one with no brakes or with an engine that would die on him after thirty or forty miles.

He rang up "No Sale" on the cash register. The last man to leave had taken all the bills, but he helped himself to change for the vending machines. He went back to the car with an armload of sandwiches, several packages of crackers, and two Styrofoam containers of coffee.

"Breakfast," he said. "Compliments of the management."

"I don't know if I'm hungry."

"And I don't know when we can stop again. You better eat."

"All right. Aren't you going to eat anything?"

"I had a pack of crackers. And I'll have some coffee."

He went back to the station and scooped the car keys off the board. He turned the ignition switch of each in turn and watched the gas gauges. Two of the cars had around half a tank each. He got a red plastic bucket from the station and rummaged around trying to find a length of hose. There was a piece of plastic tubing but it was much too short. Eventually he got a hacksaw from the work area and cut off a few yards of the air hose. Anybody who wanted to fill his tires was in for a disappointment.

He siphoned gas from the two cars. The air hose had a small diameter and the process was a slow one. He would fill the bucket, pour it into the wagon's tank, then go back and siphon some more. Each time he was unable to avoid getting a mouthful of gasoline. The taste was awful, and there was a sore spot on his lower gum that it irritated.

While he worked she sat in the car with the door closed so that the dome light would not shine. There was very little traffic on the highway. He looked up at one point to see a police car pass, probably the one he had seen at the other station. It never even slowed down.

After he had poured a final bucket of gas into the wagon, he got a can of Coke to rinse the gasoline taste out of his mouth. He kept getting a repeat of the taste, though. He went to the men's room and was sick, then drank the rest of the Coke to settle his stomach. He went back to the car just as Betty left it to use the ladies' room. While he waited for her he loaded the gun. He started to return it to the glove compartment, remembered the police car, flashed a scene of being stopped for speeding or running a light or just because the cops were bored and had nothing better to do. He saw himself agreeing to produce the license and registration, and reaching over to unlock the glove compartment, and coming up with neither the license nor the registration but with the gun, his body shielding it from the cop, and then spinning around quickly, snapping shots through the open window —

Then he began to flash all the ways it could go wrong. Better to keep the gun closer to hand. He jammed it down between the seat and the seat back and practiced reaching for it. It was in just the right place, but he kept practicing the move so that he would be familiar with it when he had to be.

She came back, got into the car beside him. She had washed her hands and face but she looked drawn, exhausted. She wanted to know more about the newscast. He went over it again as he got the car started and pulled back onto the highway.

"You can hear it yourself in a few minutes," he said. "We missed the two-thirty news but they'll have it again at three o'clock."

"I didn't know it was so late."

"You been sleeping."

"You must be exhausted yourself."

"I'm all right."

At Big Springs he turned onto Route 138 and drove southwest. The three o'clock news came on just as they crossed the Colorado line. The announcer was still calling the family Reinhart, but they had the number of victims right this time. Betty was mentioned by name, with the information that she was missing and police theorized that she had been abducted as a hostage by the killer or killers.

" 'Killer or killers,' " he said. "Told you they'd guess you were a hostage. You sure you don't want to make an escape from the killer or killers?"

She giggled, and he asked her what was so funny. "The way you said that," she said.

"Well?"

"I always want to be with you," she said.

She dozed off again, woke up when he pulled off the road to consult a Colorado road map he'd picked up at the station, then slipped back into sleep once the car was moving again. He decided to keep on following the Platte until he came to something called Brush, then head straight on south. Otherwise he'd be driving straight into Denver and he wanted to stay away from big cities. They always made him uncomfortable anyway, and now he felt their chances would be better in open country and small towns.

He started to wonder, for the first time since he had killed the man and woman in the tourist cabin, as to their ultimate destination. She had mentioned Mexico again, back at the gas station, and he wondered if that was a good idea. It seemed to him that people on the run always made for the border, one border or another, and that the police had undoubtedly figured out this particular pattern and took special pains to guard border areas. It didn't seem likely that they could patrol an entire border effectively. They would watch the roads, of course, but anyone going cross-country could likely get through. In movies set behind the Iron Curtain they always showed borders protected with miles of barbed wire and packs of guard dogs. A border of that sort would be difficult to cross, but he couldn't believe they had any comparable system of fortification between the United States and Mexico. There was a river at the border, he seemed to remember, but he also seemed to remember that the river did not form the entire boundary. They could ditch the car, cut through fields or desert or whatever they had down there, and walk right on into Mexico.

And then what the hell would they do there? She said she spoke Spanish, and he guessed a powerful number of Mexicans must speak English, and there weren't that many people he had a great urge to talk to anyway. Maybe it could work out. Some little Mex town stuck back in the hills where they never saw a newspaper or listened to a radio. Some out-of-the-way place the U.S. cops would never think to look in.

Meanwhile they would just keep running. There was a long road stretching out in front of them now, and the road he saw in his mind was even longer. He couldn't see what was at the end of it, and he thought briefly that it might not much matter what was at the end of it. The important thing was moving, moving.

The three thirty news was a repeat, word for word, of the three o'clock broadcast. There were a few more details at four o'clock — information on the Deinhardts, speculation that the killer might have had a grudge against the family.

At four thirty the sky was starting to lighten. The terrain was hilly, and the road they were on now curved in and out of the hills. The Dodge wagon had lousy shock absorbers and he had to baby it on the curves, and he kept thinking nostalgically of the Toronado. It would have straightened out those curves; it would have eaten those hills for breakfast.

The news was the same again, and he alternated between being bored at the monotony of it and grateful at the miles they were covering while the police got nowhere. Then at ten minutes to five the station cut into the middle of an old Hank Williams record with a bulletin. A ballistics check had established that the same gun which killed the Deinhardt family had been used the night before in the service station holdup. Well, he had expected that.

And five minutes after that — you would think they would wait for the five o'clock news, but no, the bastards had to show what hot stuff they were — there was another bulletin. They'd found the man and woman in the tourist cabin, and the Toronado parked out back. And he had not expected that, not so soon.

"Why are we stopping? Are we home yet?" She blinked, rubbed sleep from her eyes. He didn't answer her at first. He sat behind the wheel with his fingers tight on it. He had pulled onto the shoulder of the road and cut the ignition. Mist rose from the fields.

He couldn't think. His mind worked quickly, but it was spinning away from him and he couldn't keep a tight hold on it. That was the trouble with speed when you ran too long on it. You couldn't do that, shouldn't have to do it. If only he could have had a night's sleep in the little tourist cabin, if only he could have fitted in that many hours before the damn cops found that credit slip and made the Toronado as the holdup car. If only that dumb sonofabitch Sturdevant had made out the slip right the first time around, so that he could have taken the one slip with him and been done with it. If only —

"Jimmie John?"

"Car's no good," he said shortly.

"What's the matter with it?"

"They know about it."

"How did they —"

He turned on her. "Look, I got no time for questions. They found the other car and they must know what we're driving now, or they will in a couple hours. And besides this damn thing is a piece of shit to drive, and a station wagon's no damn good because they'll have your picture all over the place, and if we stop anywhere you'll have to hide in the trunk, and there's no fucking trunk in a fucking station wagon." He caught the expression on her face and made himself relax. "I'm sorry," he said.

"Didn't mean to snap at you. I'm all tied up in knots."

"I'm sorry."

He got out and walked around the front of the car. He couldn't open the hood, and he cursed it intently for a few moments, then checked inside the car and found a hood release switch. He got the hood up.

"What's that for?"

"We had a breakdown," he said, "and some kind soul's gonna stop to offer a helping hand."

"And then what?"

"Then we trade cars."

He got the gun, stuck it under his belt. She kept her eyes straight ahead while he did this. Then he stood in front of the car and pretended to look at the engine. For quite a while no cars passed in either direction. Then a pickup truck came by heading in the same direction as they were. There were two men in the front seat. They were dark and looked Mexican but spoke with no accent. He told them thanks all the same but he had already called the triple-A and there was a service truck on the way to them. They wished him luck and drove off.

"A station wagon is bad enough," he said. "Last thing we need is a goddamned truck."

Two cars passed without even slackening speed. Then a northbound car pulled up on the other side of the road and the driver got out. He wore a poplin windbreaker and faded Levi's and favored one leg slightly as he crossed the road toward them. His car was a Dodge Coronet. The outside was dirty with road dust, but the car looked to be fairly new.

The driver was maybe fifty-five. He had a full head of gray hair. When he smiled there were pairs of deep curved lines in his cheeks. He smiled now and said, "Reckon you got trouble."

Jimmie John said, "Not half the trouble you got."

DEAR BETTY,

I hope you don't mind me calling you Betty. But I feel I know you, even though we have never met and you do not know me.

I wrote to you once before. It was about six weeks ago. I don't know if the letter reached you or not because I did not hear from you. I know you are very busy and have no time to write but I was just wondering if you ever got my letter.

Anyway, my name is Karen Braden and I live in Wells Creek. It's a small town in the State of Washington. The nearest large city is Spokane. I am 14 and in the tenth grade.

I suppose it's silly to write and waste your time with this letter. It's just that I think about everything you have gone through and feel close to you. I think about you and Jimmie John all the time.

Could I ask you a couple of questions? I know you probably won't have time to answer this letter, but I will ask them anyhow. I know Jimmie John's favorite record was "Not Comin' Home to You," and his favorite country artist was Waylon Jennings. Could you tell me any other music he cared a lot for? Anything about his other likes and dislikes? The way he felt about things and what the two of you used to talk about? Anything you could tell me I would love to hear.

If there is anything I could do for you just let me know. Anything you need or anything like that. I guess that's about it; I can't think of anything more to write.

Very sincerely yours,
KAREN BRADEN

TWELVE

The Coronet's radio wouldn't bring in Omaha. She found a Denver station but he couldn't stand the music they played so she worked the dial until she got something he liked. Then she sat back and tried to close her eyes but they wouldn't stay shut because every time she closed them she saw things she didn't want to see.

"Pretty country," he said.

She looked out the window but couldn't make herself pay attention to the scenery. There were mountains way off to the right. She had never seen mountains before, and she was seeing them now, and she couldn't keep her mind on what she was looking at.

The worst part was when he drove the car over the dead man. That had been somehow worse than the shooting. She had not watched the shooting, but she had been unable to blot out the sound of it, two shots close together and then a third shot, and even with her eyes closed she could see what was happening in her mind. Then she looked, even though she did not want to look, and saw the man lying dead in the middle of the road and Jimmie John grabbing him by the ankles and dragging him onto the gravel shoulder.

And then he had moved the station wagon forward, parking it over the corpse. He explained it all to her. A body at the roadside would draw immediate attention, and the wagon had no trunk in which to hide the body. But the wagon itself would do a good job of hiding the body until someone took a close look at it, and a car with its hood up did not invite a close look; the average person would simply assume the car had had mechanical difficulties and the driver had gone off for assistance. Of course sooner or later some eager cop would recognize the license plate, but in the meantime they would have bought an extra couple of hours.

Something got to her, though, when the car moved forward over the dead man. She kept waiting for the wheels to pass over the corpse. She knew that he had positioned the body so that the wheels would clear it on either side, but still she braced herself for the impact that did not come. And then he loaded the gun again, very deliberately, and took the box of shells along as they got into the Coronet and turned it around and drove away.

She had a headache now, a dull throbbing ache in back of her eyes. She rubbed her forehead but the pain wouldn't quit. Her stomach rumbled and she wondered if she ought to eat something. There was a cheese sandwich left but nothing to drink, and her mouth was dry already, so that the thought of a cheese sandwich with nothing to wash it down was unappealing.

A record ended and she waited for the news. The announcer did the lead-in for a fifteen-minute summary of farm prices. She hunted for another station, then gave up and snapped the radio off and sat back.

She said, "He wanted to help us."

"Huh?"

"The man you killed. The others drove right on by, but he stopped his car because he wanted to help us, and now he's dead."

He thought it over. "It makes you wonder," he said.

"Makes you *wonder?*"

"Wasn't that what you were driving at? The bastards who go on driving, they're out of it without knowing what they missed. And this here guy who's just trying

240

to be nice, he's parked out there with a car parked over him."

A chill went through her. She crossed her arms over her chest and hugged herself. She decided not to say anything. But she had to say something.

"Why did you have to kill him?"

"You know the answer."

"To buy time."

"That's right."

"So they'll find him and this car will be bad the same as the last one."

"They'll be awhile doing it," he said. His tone was very matter-of-fact. "I took his wallet, so they'll be awhile finding out who he is and another while finding out what kind of car he was driving. Whereas if I just left him with a handshake he'd be on the phone by now. Not to mention that he was a witness."

"So am I."

"How's that?"

"I'm a witness, too, Jimmie John." Her voice was rising, but she couldn't help it. "I'm a witness, just look what a damn fine witness I am, so when are you gonna shoot me? When are you gonna —"

He hit her without even looking at her, swung a sharp backhand that caught her across the cheek. Her head slapped back

241

against the headrest. She put her hand to her face.

For another mile or so neither of them spoke a word. Then he said, "Betty, I am sorry. I never meant to do that."

"It's all right."

"Ain't all right. I never should of hit you. It's driving so much that's getting to me."

"I had no right to say what I said."

"Well, there's questions you can't ask anymore, baby. You have to know that."

"I know."

Jimmie John turned off the highway suddenly without comment, and it was almost a full minute before she realized they were on one narrow lane of dirt and gravel.

"I don't think this is a road."

He told her it was a farm road. "Farm road most often leads to a farmhouse," he said. "It's in the natural way of things."

"A farmhouse?"

"I can't drive any more. I have to crash before I run us into a tree. I'm starting to see things in front of me on the road. Cars coming at us when there aren't any cars coming at us. And we both need to wash up and eat some real food. I feel like my skin's about to crawl. There it is, big white house and a big old barn. Off on a private road like this there won't be anybody seeing the car."

He cut the engine. She looked at the house. It was a large frame structure, a sprawling house that had evidently been frequently enlarged over the years. The house was in good repair, the clapboards freshly painted, the front yard tidy, the house and walks lined with beds of daffodils just coming into bloom. There was a cow in the barnyard, and some hens. Propped against a weathered rail fence was a racing bike, and near it a child's tricycle.

Children.

"Now you wait here," he said. And she tried not to notice that he was taking the gun with him.

He got out of the car. A large yellow dog of no particular breed came trotting out from behind the house. Jimmie John slapped his thigh and the dog hurried over and let itself be scratched behind the ears. It didn't bark at all and stayed at Jimmie John's side as he walked to the side door.

She made herself think about Mexico. They would be safe in Mexico, she decided. Once they were across the border they would be all right. They wouldn't need the gun in Mexico. They could throw it away before they crossed the border, and they would never have to hurt anyone again.

Oh, God, a tricycle.

They could be very happy in Mexico. Spanish had always come easy to her, the one subject she never had any difficulty with, the one subject she actually enjoyed. And it was much much easier to learn a language, any language, when you were actually living in the country where it was spoken. You used it every day and it became second nature to you; you even thought in that language as often as you thought in English. Jimmie John didn't speak Spanish but she had enough of the language to get along for a while, and he would learn, she would help him with it, and it wouldn't be long before he spoke it as well as she did. Maybe they would speak Spanish among themselves, maybe they would actually turn into Mexicans, living in a homey little hut somewhere, raising children and —

Don't think about children.

If she were in Grand Island, it would be almost time to get up for school now. Was it a school day? Yes, it was Friday. It had been a Wednesday afternoon when they met. And now it was only Friday. It seemed impossible. Less than two days, and now four people in Grand Island were dead, and two people in the motel, and a man under the station wagon, and, and —

How many?

It would be very nice in Mexico. Maybe they would live out in the country, away from crowds and noise. Maybe they would have chickens and a cow and maybe she could learn to ride horseback, and the kids would have a burro, and —

Or the kids would have a tricycle. Maybe they should just take this tricycle for the kids, load it into the car and switch it to another car later on and, oh, God, what was happening to her?

Mexico. Think about Mexico.

"Hey!"

She opened her eyes. He was leaning against the door on her side of the car, his eyes bright.

"Never saw you like that before," he said. "Hands all knotted up and eyes squeezed tight like that. You all right?"

She nodded. She opened her hands and looked at the palms. There were semicircular indentations from her fingernails. She hadn't even known she was doing it.

"Come on in," he said. "It's a great house."

"How many?"

"How many what?"

She closed her eyes. "People."

He said, "Oh." Then he said, "Well, we got lucky for a change. Ain't nobody home. Kind of expected that, seeing as there's no car around, so I knocked some and let myself in and took the unguided tour of the place. Nobody home." His eyes narrowed. "Though by the time this gets on the damn *radio,* I guess they'll be three dead bodies in every damn room. Be a whole damn bloodbath the time they get through with it." He set his head back suddenly and laughed. "Oh, the hell," he said. "Now will you kindly come out of that car and have a look at this house I went and found for you?"

It *was* a nice house. The interior was clean and neat throughout, furnished simply but comfortably. In the front room there were homemade curtains in the windows and magazines placed precisely on the three-legged coffee table. The furniture needed dusting, but otherwise everything was immaculate. The one expensive piece of furniture in the room was a combination television-radio-stereo. There were pictures arranged on its top in matching sterling silver frames — a wedding photo of a man and woman, more recent photographs of the same two persons, and a variety of pictures of their children, some singly and some in groups. There were evidently three children, two boys and a girl, and the latest photographic evidence put the oldest boy in his early teens and the youngest around six, with the girl somewhere in the middle.

She was trying to figure out how to turn on the radio when Jimmie John came down the stairs and entered the room. "Tub and shower upstairs," he reported. "And a big old brass bed with a mattress that about swallows you up. Turn that off, why don't you."

"I thought you might want to hear the news."

"I don't want to hear so much as a syllable for the next eight hours. Makes no difference what's on the news. Whatever they say, we're gonna do the same thing. Namely shower and eat and get some sleep."

"Suppose they come home while we're sleeping?"

"They won't come home."

For a moment she thought he meant that they were dead, that he had killed them after all and dragged their corpses to the cellar to spare her feelings. Then he said, "You got to learn to read signs. See how there's a layer of dust on everything? This is a neat woman who lives here. The way she keeps this house you know she's not the kind to go without dusting. Plus I looked at the refrigerator, and there's nothing in it but things that wouldn't spoil. No milk, no vegetables, no meat. They're on a trip, it looks to me."

"They'll have to come back sometime."

"It won't be today." He took hold of her shoulders. "Here's something else," he said. "All the farmhouses in the state of Colorado and we came to this one. First one we so much as took a look at, and not a soul around. Now you don't often find a farmhouse where everybody's gone. Too many things need doing every day. My guess is something came up sudden that they had to pull the kids out of school and everybody pile in the car. Say a death in the family and they all had to go to the funeral. So they make arrangements for someone to come by and milk the cow and throw some corn to the hens, and away they go.

"And as for them coming back, it won't be today. It was meant for us to come to this particular house, maybe the only one in the county with nobody home. And the same thing that made it happen that way is gonna keep them from coming home today, and besides they wouldn't come home at the beginning of a weekend, would they? They'll be home Sunday night and not before."

"Maybe it really was meant for us to come here."

"Hell, didn't I *say* it was? I'll get the car out of sight in case some neighbor comes around before we're out of here. That cow's bag is down so the morning milkin's already been done, but you never know who's gonna wander by."

"How did you notice about the cow?"

"Just happened to take it in. Why?"

"Oh, the way you notice things. I saw the dust and all and didn't think."

"Oh, you'd of thought it through for yourself in another couple of minutes," he said. But she saw his face and saw he was proud of himself and pleased with her praising him.

He let her shower first. She waited in bed while he showered and shaved. When he joined her she said she didn't think she could sleep.

"Because of sleeping all that time in the car."

"That kind of sleep doesn't do you any

good. Real sleep in a real bed is what a person needs. How do you like the bed?"

"It's so soft. I wish —"

"What?"

"I was just thinking I wished someday we could have a bed like this."

"Someday maybe we will. Let me get you a glass of water."

"I'm not thirsty."

"No, to swallow these. Or better you just take one, not being used to them."

"What are they?"

"Reds. They help you sleep. Go ahead, don't be afraid of it. I'll never give you anything that's bad for you. I took two, but one's all you'll need."

She washed the pill down with a sip of water. The water was very cold, with a slight mineral taste that she did not find at all objectionable. He went downstairs to make sure all the lights were off, then came back upstairs and got into bed beside her.

They made love. Slowly, gently, and toward the end the sleeping pill began to work and lent a dreamy slow-motion quality to the act. He used his hands on her for a long time, and then he took her, and when he shuddered and gasped on top of her a feeling of infinite peace went through her entire body.

There was a moment, between love-making and sleep, when bad thoughts began to come to her. But her mind was dull and the thoughts were wispy and formless, and before she could grab onto any of them everything slid out from under her and she slept.

She awoke frightened, unsure where she was, unable to distinguish reality from a ragged dream of pursuit. She lay still, her body cradled in the deep soft mattress, her face pressed into her pillow, and was afraid to open her eyes. She waited until she knew for certain just where she was and just what had happened.

Eyes open, she blinked at sunlight streaming through the chintz curtains. She was alone in the bedroom, and her first thought was that he had left her. Then she thought that he wouldn't just leave her, that he would shoot her first, and she bit her lip fiercely, furious with herself for such disloyalty.

She walked to the doorway and called his name.

"Thought you'd sleep all day, girl."

"What time is it?"

"Getting on for three o'clock. For

someone who didn't think she could sleep, you made a good stab at it."

"I guess I was tired."

"Well, throw some clothes on and get down here. Did you mean it when you said you knew how to cook? You got a chance to prove it."

He had found bacon in the freezer and had time to thaw it, and fresh eggs stolen still warm from nests in the barn. The eggs came out a little rubbery, but he praised her cooking extravagantly and asked for more. She couldn't figure out how to work the percolator but found a jar of instant coffee and made cups for both of them. They drank it black with sugar. She had always had coffee with cream in it, but discovered now that it was better without.

He had done some exploring while she slept. In the basement he found an old Maytag washing machine and a gas dryer, and after they had eaten she climbed down a steep flight of steps and loaded all their dirty clothes into the machine. While the clothes washed she sat with him in the front room. He had found a large leather-bound family photo album, and they sat together on the sofa and went through it, making up stories about the people in the photographs.

"Now this fellow here, he's the bad uncle, the sumbitch nobody else can tolerate. See, he never amounted to much, you can just tell by those shifty little eyes there, but that one girl a couple of pages back, she was the ugly sister like we decided, and nobody else would marry her."

"So he married her and the rest of the family can't stand him but they put up a front for poor Jessica's sake."

"That's just what they do. Have to put up with Tom to make old Jessie happy."

"And he treats her terrible."

"No, he treats her pretty good, actually, but he treats everybody else bad, and he's so shiftless you can't do a thing with him. They all think he married her for her money, but he actually does love her, for all that he's a bad sumbitch to everybody else."

"And she's the only one who appreciates his true virtues."

"Old Jessie, she's a real appreciator. But everybody else, well, old Tom's the sort that borrows your lawnmower and brings it back rusted."

"If he brings it back at all."

"Oh, no question, you have to ask him and ask him, and then he brings it back, like he's doing you the most almighty favor, and sure it's rusted and the blades is nicked from gravel and like as not the belt's broken. That's Tom for you every time. Why you laughing?"

"You're funny."

"You think I'm funny, just have a look at Aunt Alice. Here she is admiring a bed of roses. Now Aunt Alice is just the sweetest little old lady you'd care to meet. I suppose you can see that."

"Well, she certainly looks the part."

"She surely does, and on top of it Aunt Alice isn't all there. You know, she has like a faraway look in her eyes, and when you get in a conversation with her, which you don't do when you got any choice in the matter, she sort of focuses a few feet in back of your head, and if you put a question to her you'll get an answer, but it might not be what you had in mind. Like you'll say something to the effect of asking her what time it is, and she'll say as to how it's sure to be a cold winter because the birds are heading south earlier than usual."

"Did Aunt Alice ever get married?"

"There was a fellow who always wanted to marry her, but there was this rumor that he had nigger blood in him, so she would never go through with it. Now the rest of the family thinks Aunt Alice is still a virgin."

"But she isn't?"

"Hell, no. That fellow who wanted to marry her, he comes to see her every September when the moon is full. She sneaks him up to her room and they do what they do."

"Does she ever get pregnant?"

"Every damn time. But as plump as she is it doesn't show too much, and each spring she hatches another little bastard and keeps him hidden away in her closet until he's a year old. Then she wrings his little neck and digs a hole in the garden and plants a rosebush over him. That's why she manages to raise these prize-winning roses."

"Why does she keep doing that?"

"Well, she's not what you'd call all there, Aunt Alice. She's not a hundred percent all present and accounted for. And the thing is, see, she loves babies, but she just can't abide children."

"Maybe one of these days she'll get one she likes enough to keep."

"You'd think so, but the fact is that Aunt Alice was one hundred and fourteen years old last August, and she doesn't have too many childbearing years ahead of her."

"Then instead of saying she can't abide children, you'll be able to say she can't bear them."

"Oh, girl. Now I'm going to be a true gentleman and make pretend I never heard you say that."

In the kitchen, with him sitting in one chair with his feet on another and drinking a cup of coffee while she folds the clean clothes and packs them into their bags. In the front room on the sofa, his arm around her, her head on his shoulder, just sitting with no need to say a word. Up in the bedroom, in the soft cocoon of a bed, touching and tickling and kissing, playing like kittens.

"Jimmie John? I wish today could go on forever. I wish we could stay here for the rest of our lives."

"Me too."

"You know, I was never alive before."

"You were pretty lively couple of minutes ago."

"I was never a person. You made a person out of me."

"You were more person than you ever knew."

"I just love being with you." And turning to him, staring hard to hold tears back: "I

256

don't care, I don't care what happens, no matter what happens. I'll always be glad I walked out of that movie and you were there. Always. Even if —"

"Easy now."

"Even if they catch up with us —"

"They won't."

"But even if they do."

"They won't."

Late in the afternoon she asked him if he wanted to hear a newscast.

"Not here," he said. "Not in this house. You know what I'm getting at?"

"Yes."

"I want everything to be right in this house. Time enough when we leave. Oh, I could tell you right now what they're gonna say. Back on the road, though, I'll keep that radio on, listen to it, hear the same damn thing over and over again. But not here."

"I know."

A couple of times, sitting silently at his side, she played with a pretty little daydream. The Chitterton family — they had learned the name from a drawer full of bills in the sideboard in the dining room — would never return to the farm. In the first version of the reverie she had them annihilated in an auto accident, but she subsequently revised this, eliminating the tragic element and having Mr. Chitterton find a uranium mine or take a fantastic job offer or inherit a fortune and take his family on a world cruise. Whatever the circumstances, the Chittertons would never return, and she and Jimmie John would be able to stay there for the rest of their lives.

The police would never think to look for them there. The neighbors would keep their distance like good gentle countryfolk, simply assuming that she and Jimmie John had bought the place from the Chittertons.

Every morning and every night she would go out to milk the cow, and in the mornings she would accompany him to gather the fresh-laid eggs. They would stuff themselves on huge country breakfasts and spend long afternoons walking in the fields and picking fruit from their own trees. In a few years there would be a boy of their own riding that tricycle she had seen. They would live out their lives surrounded by their children and their animals and the sky and the trees and the flowers, until she was as old and dotty as Aunt Alice in the family photo album, and when they died years and years from now they would be buried on their own land, under their own piece of sky.

An hour after sunset he touched her arm and she knew. She looked at him and he nodded.

"Can I take a look around before we go?"

"I got to get the car anyway."

She walked through the rooms of the old house. She would never forget these rooms; if she lived a hundred years she would be able to sketch them from memory. Everything they had touched had been returned to its proper place, every dish and spoon washed and dried and put back where it came from. In fact they were leaving the house better than they had found it, for she had spent a good hour going from room to room with a dustcloth. Mrs. Chitterton was an immaculate housekeeper and shouldn't have to return to dust-filled tabletops.

She waited for him in the front hall. He walked past her into the kitchen and she followed him. He said, "For the food we used and all," and put some money on the table.

"Should we leave a note?"

"I don't know. What do you think?"

"Otherwise they won't know where the money came from, and they might be confused." She got a pencil and a small scrap of paper from beside the telephone and printed: *"This is for the food we ate and to show we appreciate your hospitality."*

She tapped the point of the pencil against a front tooth and looked up at him. "Should I sign it?"

"No sense putting our names or nothing."

She printed: YOUR SECRET FRIENDS.

They weren't on the road ten minutes before a newscast came on. Jimmie John seemed to take it all in stride, but it scared her, hearing it all like that. They knew his name now from fingerprints left behind at her parents' house. They had found the man under the station wagon. They knew about the Coronet they were driving now.

"Took this car for nothing," he said philosophically. "If I'd of known, but at the time I didn't figure on stopping so soon. Time to trade it in."

But this time he planned more carefully. He parked the car on the shoulder at a bend in the road. There was a steep drop into a boulder-strewn ravine just a few yards from the side of the road.

The Coronet's glove compartment provided a couple of emergency flares and a flashlight. He set up the flares and stood out in the middle of the road with the flashlight, and the first car that came along had the choice of stopping or running him down. The car stopped and the driver rolled down his window and Jimmie John shot him.

He stuffed the dead man, minus his wallet, into the Coronet's trunk. He unbolted the license plates from the Coronet and tossed them, along with their bags, into the trunk of the new car. Then he got the Coronet running and walked along beside it, steering it, then jumping nimbly out of the way while it went the rest of the way over the cliff.

The noise was shattering. She closed her eyes at the sound, opened them to see Jimmie John standing at the cliff looking down at the wreck.

"C'mon," he was saying. "Go ahead and *burn,* you son of a bitch."

Seconds later she heard the explosion. Flames leaped from the wrecked Coronet. He turned to her with satisfaction, took her arm, got her into the new car.

"Now just let 'em piss up a rope," he said. "Let 'em try to identify that poor bastard, assuming they so much as find him. The hell, be a few days before they even know that's the Dodge they're lookin' for, and here we are in a what-is-it, a Pontiac, and do you want to know something? This time we did it, Betty. This time we're gonna be a couple thousand miles out of here without them having the slightest notion of what happened to us." He slapped his leg. "Hey, girl — we made it!"

She put the radio on and found a station with their kind of music. An hour later there was another bit of news. A rancher in Texas had turned up the body of Walker P. Ferris, and the medical examiner had established the cause of death as repeated blows to the head with a blunt instrument.

She didn't say anything. After a while he said, "I could tell you it was bullshit about the cause of death and how he had a heart attack and I knew he was dead and left him in a field because I couldn't afford to get in trouble with the law. But the hell with all that. It's like they said."

She nodded.

"Make you mad?"

"No," she said.

And it didn't. Because, for one thing, she had already taken it for granted that he

had killed Ferris. And because, for another, she no longer cared how many
strangers had to die. She knew she should
care but she didn't, not now. The day they
had just spent was worth all those lives.

"I get goose bumps just thinking about it. And what you folks must be feeling."

"Well, you can't imagine."

"Were you frightened?"

"It wasn't a question of being frightened at the time, because we had no way of knowing who it was and all then. But sometimes now I will be thinking of something else and it will come up on me unawares and I will just about faint away. Can't help thinking what could have happened and all."

"We're not safe in our own homes, not a one of us."

"No sooner did I open the door than I knew someone had been inside. Don't ask me how I knew."

"Sometimes you just know things."

"Tom says maybe there's a sixth sense operating in cases like this."

"There's a lot we don't understand in

this world, is what I always say."

"I walked in and I thought at first someone was still there, and I told Tom and he called out and there was no answer and he said I was just being silly, what with being exhausted from the trip, and he went on in and turned lights on and all. And I knew someone had been inside and gone. If you ask what was different, I don't believe I could say. You might think it was something was moved around or something of the sort, but you know as well as I do, when there's children in a house nothing's in the same place all the time. Like you might think a china pitcher was always kept on the left-hand side of the breakfront and it turns out one of the children moved it to set up a checkerboard or what-all. Then I went in the kitchen and saw the note and the money and like to fainted."

"It was true about them leaving money, then."

"Almost a hundred dollars. The note said it was to pay for what they ate, but if they ate five dollars' worth of anything I would be hard put to prove it. And do you know how the note was signed?"

"Something about secret friends?"

" 'Your secret friends.' Tom just laughed

and said as to how our secret friends could come back again paying out sums like that, and he took and put the money in his wallet without a by-your-leave. I'll tell you, I felt pretty strange at the thought of strangers coming into my house when I was gone, but we talked it over and decided it was some college students on a vacation or something, and maybe they had car trouble and had to put up over-night."

"But when you found out —"

"Oh, Lord. I still get the shivers."

"Just your good fortune you weren't home."

"Well, I would surely say so. But you know, I wonder if they were all as bad as they're painted. Tom thinks I'm crazy for saying as much, but I can't help but wonder. Not stealing a thing, and leaving money when they didn't have to, and I tell you, they washed up the dishes and left the place as neat as you could ask. I know they did what they did and all but I wonder isn't there more to them than we know."

"I still say you'd have been murdered in your beds if you were home when they came."

"Maybe so. I just don't know. Do you want to know something? I just think it's a shame Tom picked up that money and tucked it away, all mixed in with his own so there was no way of telling it apart. It's silly, a dollar being a dollar, but I wish I could have kept that money apart for a souvenir."

"You have the note, don't you?"

"Oh, I wouldn't take anything for that note. I'll get a little frame for it next I get to town, if I don't forget."

THIRTEEN

There were moments when it felt as though he had been driving forever, as though he had been born at the wheel of a car some hundreds and hundreds of years ago and would spend eternity driving through this dark void. They sped south through Colorado toward the New Mexico line. They drove miles at a time without seeing a single light except for an occasional oncoming car. For most of the time clouds obscured the moon, and the black asphalt pavement seemed to absorb the headlight beams and reflect nothing. For a couple of hours the radio babbled, music and news, music and news, until he couldn't take any more of it and turned it off. It was nothing but records he had heard a thousand times, broken every half hour by the same damned news items, over and over and over. Ordinarily he could tune out the music and the news as well, but tonight it was impossible.

It was an irritant, and he seemed to be irritating easily now.

With the radio off, the silence was even worse. He almost turned the damn thing back on again. Betty sat motionless in her seat, barely speaking at all, and for his part he kept wanting a conversation to get started but didn't know how to put it in gear.

He would say that it was a hell of a dark night and she would agree that it certainly was. Or she would say that a certain hill was a pretty steep one and he would grunt his assent. He sort of wished she would talk to him. It wouldn't even matter what she said, if only she could launch into a nice loose monologue that he could just float along with. But you couldn't ask a person to talk to you without being prepared to talk back in return.

His mind kept flashing back to that farmhouse. How happy they had been there and all, as if they'd stepped smack into another world. And how she had wanted the day to go on forever, how she'd hoped to spend a lifetime there without ever seeing another person but him.

The more he thought of it, the more pleased he was that he had thought to leave money behind. It surely hadn't hurt him to do it. Lately it seemed that they kept accumulating money and having precious little opportunity to spend any. He'd left a hundred dollars for the Chittertons, which, all things considered, was a fairly steep price for some eggs and bacon and coffee, but he liked the idea that someone whose path had crossed theirs had profited by the experience. God knew enough of them had lost.

He thought about the most recent victim, tucked into the Coronet trunk and shoved over a cliff and fried to a cinder. It would slow the cops down, all right. Give them a little breathing space for now.

He had told her they were home free now. And wondered if she believed him.

He hoped she did. She had been so happy at that farmhouse, and he wanted her to be happy as much of the time as she could. Because as far as he could see there was no way they could get completely out of this.

There were just too many dead people scattered all over the place, and together they threw up so much heat that you could never expect it to die down. Crossing a state line did you about as much good as crossing a street, and as far as a national border — maybe it was just his mood now, tired and wrapped up into his own self, sad at leaving the farmhouse, but he couldn't see Mexico for dust. They'd have helicopters out for sure, and every border patrol would be well supplied with pictures of the two of them.

He hadn't even known they had a picture of him in their files. It had to be an old one, a couple of years at the least, and he couldn't even remember the last time someone with a badge had pointed a camera in his direction. But then it didn't have to look too much like him. There just had to be enough of a resemblance to get some cop interested, and then there was nothing to do but try and get out of it alive, and if you managed that it bought you a ticket to run some more until you went through the whole thing all over again.

It would all be worth it, she had said. Even if they were caught, even then, it would all be worth it.

Well, she'd probably get the chance to find out if it really was.

He stomped the gas pedal involuntarily and the car shot forward. She started and asked what was the matter, and he told her nothing was the matter, just a shadow at the roadside.

He took deep breaths and kept his eyes

on the road and pushed things around inside his head. He wasn't going to think those thoughts any more. They made him feel bad, they took the fine sheer edge off him, and besides they weren't true.

Just no way they could be true.

Because as long as you did the right things and made the right choices you got out all right. That farmhouse, for example. What was the odds against finding a farmhouse first shot out of the box with nobody home? Hundred to one? Thousand to one? But that was what they did, proving he was still on top of things, still swimming with the tide, and because of that they had had the best day of their lives and the Chittertons were a hundred dollars to the good.

If the Chittertons had been home, they wouldn't have that hundred dollars. Instead they'd all be dead. But he was damned if he was going to think about that now. There was just no percentage in it.

A few miles into New Mexico he looked at the gas gauge for the first time in too long. The needle was smack on the big *E.* He couldn't remember the last time he'd seen a gas station, open or shut. And God knew he couldn't afford to wait for a closed one.

Wouldn't *that* just do it. Finally having a really clean car and having to switch cars because he'd been fool enough to run the tank dry.

He cut the ignition, put the car in neutral and let her roll. Might as well get every extra yard out of what he had left.

"What's the matter?"

"We're damn near out of gas is what's the matter."

"Where's the station? I don't see it."

"I don't goddamn know where the station is. I don't spend that much time in New goddamn Mexico." He got a grip on himself and said, "Can't be two of us in the car if I do find a station. And your picture's sure to be in all the papers by now. I'm putting you in the trunk."

"I'm afraid."

"Huh?"

"You put him in the trunk. The last one."

"You rather I let you out and come back for you? Do that if you want, but I might drive ten miles and run out of gas and then how the hell do we find each other?"

"No, I'll get in the trunk."

"Not if you can't handle it."

273

"I'll be all right."

She got out of the car. He opened the trunk and she hesitated just an instant before climbing up and in. Now it was getting to him; he was being psyched by what she had said. Every image he flashed was a bad one.

"You'll be right in the car, won't you?"

"All the time."

"Don't leave me or anything."

He reached for the trunk lid and flashed coffin lids slamming shut, flashed shovelfuls of earth tossed into open graves. He almost told her to get out and chance recognition, preferring the chance of having to gun down an attendant to locking her up like that.

"I'm okay, honey."

He threw the lid shut and got back behind the wheel.

He drove almost twenty miles before he found a station. He babied the remaining gas supply all the way, taking downgrades in neutral, driving throughout like a contender in a miles-per-gallon derby.

The old man who filled the tank dragged one leg as he walked, and one arm hung loose at his side. He wore a hunter's jacket and a red plaid cap and spoke only once, to name the amount of the sale. Jimmie

John paid him and drove off without waiting for change, and a couple of hundred yards down the road he stopped and let her out of the trunk.

"Wasted effort," he said. "You coulda been not only up front but stark naked and that old fart never woulda known the difference. He walked like this."

She giggled.

"Sorry I made you do that. You all right?"

"Seemed like it lasted forever. But then I got so I was happy about it. Oh, it'll sound silly, but I was thinking how you do everything, you know, and I'm just sort of along, and for a change I was doing something, and I was glad I had the chance to do it."

When the sun came up he braked the car to a stop. She looked troubled. He put a hand on her leg and told her everything was all right.

"I just wanted a minute to look at all that," he said. "Big old sun coming up over the desert. All those colors, reds and purples. Nothing out there but sand and rock, and will you just look at the colors they put up when the sun hits them. Never seen anything like it."

"Have you ever been in this part of the country before?"

"Maybe."

"Don't you remember?"

He went on gazing out his window. At length he said, "Well, I'm not a hundred percent sure. I know I never saw what I'm looking at now. I guess I been through here, all right. Maybe by night or in the middle of the day, or maybe I wasn't tuned into things and never took a long look around. Some people go their whole lives that way, never seeing what they're looking at. Even the air is different out here. Makes you want to breathe more than usual. Damn, you can see for miles, and everywhere you look there's something worth looking at."

"It's . . . like a movie."

He put his head back and laughed. "You know," he said, "it's just exactly that. So real it looks like a picture. You look off over there and can't you just see some old cowboy riding like hell? Hat tossed back and spurs digging into his horse, and way off in back of him a column of dust coming up showing the posse's after him? See it?"

"Will they catch him?"

"Nobody catches old Trevor Cole. Not so long as he's up there on his faithful steed. Damn if I can recollect the name of his faithful steed."

"His faithful steed is a golden palomino."

"Old Trevor wouldn't have nothing else. A golden palomino and his name is Tornado 'cause he's fast as the wind."

"Why are they after him?"

"Oh, let me figure. Robbed a bank? No, Trevor wouldn't rob no bank. Let's see now. Well, old Trevor went back home and found out his old widowed mother got chased off the ancestral homestead by a sumbitch mining company. So he robbed the stage and took off their whole gold shipment and gave it to the poor folks and the Indians."

"Does he have a faithful Indian companion?"

"Did. Had a sidekick named Pronto, but the sumbitch posse got him way off back of those hills. Nobody left but Trevor and Tornado. That puts me in mind of that car. Tornado and Toronado. Well, old Tornado, he's got front-wheel drive his own self. No posse gonna catch up with him."

She didn't answer. He turned to look at her and saw tears in her eyes. He said, "Hey, girl," and the tears began to flow. He kissed her and her hands dug into his shoulders.

After awhile she said she was all right. She straightened up and wiped her eyes dry. "I don't know what it was," she told him. "Just how beautiful it is here, I guess."

"And running all this time, and not enough sleep."

"I guess."

"Not to mention you must be hungry. I shoulda got some sandwiches when we got gas but I didn't want to leave you in the trunk."

"I'm all right."

"I'll get us some carry-out next place I see. You won't have to get in the trunk again, if that's what you were thinking. It's different at a gas station where somebody comes right up to the car. Probably be some sort of restaurant coming up in the next couple of miles."

"Where are we?"

"New Mexico."

"Well, I knew that."

"It's about as much as I know myself. Never paid much attention to the last few places we went through. Just went right on through 'em without taking time out to read. Remind me I got to get some bullets."

"Bullets?"

"Uh-huh. Just a couple left besides what's in the gun, and tomorrow's Sunday, meaning the stores'll be closed."

She didn't say anything until the car was rolling again. Then she said, "I thought we were safe now."

"Since we got this car? I'd say we're a whole lot safer than we used to be."

"I thought we wouldn't have to, you know."

"Keep on running?"

"No, I know we have to do that."

"Because we ain't in no place that it's safe to stay in for long."

"I know that. I meant, oh, we wouldn't have to shoot anybody any more."

"Hope we don't."

She didn't say anything.

"Hope we don't," he repeated. "Same as old Trevor, I know there's no posse gonna catch us. But old Trevor, you don't see him throwing his gun away. Even with Tornado going like hell under him, he's still keeping that six-gun on his hip."

The glorification of the criminal . . . is deeply rooted in all of Western civilization, with one version or another of the Robin Hood myth extant throughout European culture. In America the tendency finds perhaps its fullest expression. The popular mind endows Dillinger with a twenty-two-inch penis and depicts Pretty Boy Floyd as a friend to the poor. Willie Sutton appears on television endorsing a bank credit card; Arnold Schuster, responsible for his capture, was regarded as a betrayer, and his murder . . . aroused little popular outcry.

One wonders if it is not our sense of drama which endows the criminal with a heroism he does not possess. Innocent victims, after all, are not the stuff mythology is made of, nor does a methodical police bureaucracy enlist our sympathies. Whatever his true motives, whatever the real nature of his character, we prefer to cast the criminal as a lone rebel warring against a world he never made. . . . And now, in an age in which the solitary heroics of a Lindbergh have given way to the mechanistic collective effort of moon shots, where warfare is the province of ignorant armies who clash by computer technology, the criminal is very nearly the only hero left to us.

It is not entirely surprising, then, that criminals have grown to believe the myths created about them.

— J. Donald Goerlander,
The Villain as Victim

I know some day they will gun them down
And bury them side by side
To some it will be grief,
   to the law a big relief
But it's death for Bonnie and Clyde
          — Bonnie Parker

FOURTEEN

The sign for the Apache Tears Trading Post enumerated its offerings — Mexican and American cuisine, souvenirs, beer, package goods, mineral specimens, Navaho crafts. When they reached the place it seemed too small for all it provided. It was a square adobe building with a flat plank roof set fifty yards off the road in back of a large gravel parking area. There was a gas station opposite and a tavern diagonally across the intersection. He parked a good distance away from the half dozen other cars.

"You can hunch down in the seat a little," he told her. "I'll leave the motor running just in case we have to go somewhere in a hurry."

The impact of his words didn't register until he had already disappeared inside the trading post. Then she began to tremble. The Pontiac idled hard, the engine shaking the body slightly, and now she felt as though the barely perceptible movement was shaking her to pieces.

Just in case we have to go somewhere in a hurry. Just in case someone recognized him, or somehow made trouble. Just in case he had to yank that terrible gun out of his belt and kill more people. Or had he left the gun? She checked where he kept it, between seat and seat back, and it was gone. Of course he would have it with him, and for much the same reason that he had left the motor running. He couldn't afford to take chances.

She kept bracing herself for the sound of gunfire. But would she hear it if it came? The building was a ways off, the door closed. She stared at the door and kept waiting for Jimmie John to burst through it, a smoking gun in his hand, racing to the car. And her mind kept throwing up ways things could go wrong. Suppose the engine stalled right now? Suppose it cut out and cost him valuable time when he ran from the building? Would she know how to get it started again?

The door opened, and she tensed, and someone else emerged with his arms full of packages. He got into a blue Ford, backed up in a wide arc, drove away.

The door opened three more times as

other people left the place. Each time she tightened up, and each time she was able to relax a little more completely, telling herself that there would likely be no trouble if there had been none so far.

She put on the radio. He didn't seem to want to hear it, but she could turn it off when he came back. She worked her way around the dial quickly without hitting a newscast, then as quickly turned the radio off again.

When the door opened she did not recognize him at first. A large brown paper sack obscured him from the waist almost to his eyes, and those eyes were covered by a pair of dark wraparound sunglasses. But it was him, and he was walking quickly but not hurriedly, moving with confidence, and she let out a breath she had not realized she was holding.

In the car he said, "You know, I bought these without so much as thinking about a disguise. Bright as the sun is, I thought they'd rest my eyes some on the road. Then I thought again and got a pair for you. Here they are. I'll tell you, I won't say I wouldn't know you myself, but they do a powerful job of hiding you. You take 'em off every once in awhile, will you? I'd hate to forget what your eyes look like."

"I can just close my eyes and know what your eyes look like."

"Mean and beady."

"Oh, no."

He grinned. "I got us food enough for a month," he said. "Sandwiches and Cokes and a mess of candy bars. They even had these little packages of dried beef like old Trevor eats on when he's hiding out up in the mountains. I got us a mess of them. I figure we might as well fill up right across the way. Let him check the oil, too. Engine's been sounding funny. Nobody's gonna look at you twice with the sunglasses on. You might even go to the ladies' room, freshen up a bit. Reason I was so long, I had a quick shave in the men's room there. They had one of those machines sells you everything you could think of. Puzzles and key chains and rubbers and aspirin. Toothbrush, toothpaste. I put in a couple of quarters and got a little plastic razor with a blade in it. Blade might of been plastic too for the shave I got, but I hate looking sloppy."

"You look fine."

"I've had closer shaves, but it'll do. He's coming to my side of the car so you get out your side and just walk right on over to the ladies' room. You see where it's at?" He leaned his head out of the window. "Fill her with the high test," he said, "and maybe have a look under the hood."

Back on the road he said, "Had a stack of papers at the store there. Albuquerque and El Paso, Texas. Had your picture right up on page one of the El Paso paper. Tell you, it didn't look a whole lot like you. I guess somebody might recognize you from that picture, but he'd be going some to do it."

"How come you didn't buy a paper?"

"That anxious to see yourself? Now that you're a celebrity? I guess you'll be wanting to keep a scrapbook next."

"No, I just —"

"Thing is, they had a picture of me, too."

"Oh."

"I should of got it just so you could have a good laugh over it. Must be five years ago they took it. I got picked up, you know, for borrowing a car, but I got off. Meantime they gave me one of their haircuts and took my picture." He laughed. "Hair all of a quarter-inch all the way around, and I'm looking about fourteen years old in that picture, and the expression on my face, I must have been scared to hell when they snapped that picture. I don't guess it looks much like me now."

"I wish I could see it."

"Do you? I guess you will sometime or other. What I thought, though, is I buy a paper and it just might put somebody in mind of taking a long look at me *and* at that picture, and looking from one to another you might see the resemblance. Sandwich okay?"

"Uh-huh."

"I got every kind they had to make sure of finding something you'd like."

"It's very good," she said.

"I could eat one of those Clark bars," he said, "if you'd unwrap it and hand it to me."

She was groping for a candy bar when she found the necklace. It was a piece of cord strung with round pebbles half an inch in diameter. They were smooth as glass, cool to the touch. Most of them were black, with some a dark gray.

"For you," he said. "Oh, it's no big deal. They're what they call Apache tears. They come all polished like that. There's a story goes with 'em that the Apache women used to cry when their men were killed in battle, and then their tears would turn to stone. Because they were so brave or I don't know what. That necklace wasn't but a couple of dollars, so I guess those

Apache women did a lot of crying."

She worked the catch, fastened the string of glossy stones around her neck.

"It's beautiful," she said.

"Well, I thought because of the story, and that place being called the Apache Tears Post. Trading Post. Doesn't look like much. Thought it was black glass beads at first. Actually there was volcanoes years ago and that's where they came from."

"I like the story about the Apache women better."

"It does make a good story."

"I think it's true. They cried and their tears turned to stone. Is it okay if I believe it?"

"You believe what you want, baby. I'll believe it, too, if you want."

She touched the stones at her throat, learned their shapes with her fingers. She was not a Catholic, but the image that came to her was of nuns saying their rosaries.

There had been times, a couple of years ago, when the idea of becoming a nun had not been without appeal to her. She had pictured herself cloaked in black, spending years and years deep within the convent walls, devoting herself to service, never hearing a loud voice. Around that time she had occasionally imagined that Judy might have become a nun. It did not seem impossible then that Judy might have experienced a profound religious feeling that could have led her to such a turn.

She thought of Judy now, and wondered how her sister really corresponded to the several pictures she'd formed of her over the past few years. Judy in a nun's habit, a stewardess' uniform, a nurse's starched white clothing. All of those images, so easily held so long in the mind, now refused to stay in focus. Because there really was no Judy any more. Not in her life, not really. Judy had been gone from her for six years, and in a sense Judy had ceased to exist outside of her own mind, where she had been free to draw Judy's picture any way she wanted.

"I didn't stop wanting that Clark bar, Betty."

"Oh," she said. "I'm sorry." And reached into the bag to get it for him.

In a city called Roswell he said, "Sporting goods store."

"Do we want sporting goods?"

"Bullets. Shells for the gun."

She had forgotten.

"Right in the middle of town, though."

He kept on driving. "Be happier with one on the outskirts."

"Why?"

"Just easier is all. I like to do my stopping on the edge of something so I can be right on out of it when I'm done."

"Oh."

He drove through the city to its southern edge, then circled around to the western side and explored first one commercial street and then another. The city reminded her of Grand Island, although she couldn't say why. It looked to be larger, and the buildings were nothing like buildings in Grand Island, all of them constructed of adobe and topped with flat roofs.

"There was one."

"A store?"

"On your side. Passed it. Shit. We'll go around the block and park right in front."

They circled the block and there was a parking space almost directly in front of the store. Mort's Sport Shop, with fishing rods and rifles in the window. On its right was a laundromat, a narrow storefront with rows of washers and dryers. On its left someone named Michael Moscato dealt in real estate and insurance.

"Won't be long. You might get down in the seat a little."

She sat still for a minute or two after he had gotten out of the car. She felt thirsty then, and got a can of Coke from the bag. She was struggling with the ring-top opener when she saw the policemen out of the corner of her eye. There were two of them, tall lean men in gray uniforms and tooled boots and broad-brimmed Western-style hats. They had come up the sidewalk behind her.

She absolutely froze. She wanted to turn her face away from them but couldn't stop watching them. At first she was sure they were coming to the car, and then when they continued on past her she knew they would enter the sporting goods store. Maybe the proprietor had stepped on a button that would summon them. Or maybe they were just looking to pick up a hunting rifle, and they would walk in the door and Jimmie John would see them and —

It seemed to her that they paused when they were abreast of the entrance to the store. But then, magically, they were walking as before, walking on past the sporting goods store, walking down the broad street away from her.

She couldn't seem to get her breath. She looked at the palms of her hands. They glistened with sweat. She rubbed them against the front of her skirt but couldn't get them dry, couldn't get any warmth into her hands. She looked up again and the cops were nearing the corner.

Just as they started to cross the street, she heard the gunshot.

The cops heard it, too. She stared dry-mouthed as one of them took the other by the arm, turned him around. It seemed to her that both of them were staring straight at her. They just stood in their tracks for what seemed like forever.

She thought. *Just a car backfiring. That's all it was, damn you, just a car backfiring or a truck, not a gunshot, so turn around again and walk away, walk away, keep walking, please turn around and walk away —*

They were walking toward her now. Toward her. Toward the store. Not in a hurry but with a curious calm deliberation, as if they knew perfectly well that what they had heard had been nothing more ominous than a backfiring engine, but still resolved to go through the motions of investigation.

She managed to draw a breath. The motor was running, and there was no car parked immediately in front of them. If he came out now he could have the car in motion before they figured out what was happening. They were on foot; they couldn't come after them.

What was he waiting for?

Then a second gunshot, and a third.

There could be no mistaking them for backfires. The cops had recognized them as gunfire and knew where they had come from. She watched as they sprinted to within thirty yards of the storefront. One had his gun drawn, the other was reaching for his.

And Jimmie John appeared in the doorway.

"Cops, Jimmie John! There!"

She had her head out of the window and she was yelling and pointing, and one of the cops was looking in her direction, his attention momentarily divided, and the other cop was shooting, and she heard glass break as his bullet starred a store window. He fired again and missed again and Jimmie John was down on one knee, the revolver held at arm's length, and she saw the gun buck in his hand and the cop fall. He lay on his back and didn't move.

Now the other cop was shooting. A bullet chipped the pavement a dozen yards behind Jimmie John. Jimmie John aimed, and he seemed to be taking forever, and the cop was snapping off one shot after another, all of them wide, and Jimmie John fired and the cop went down with a bullet in his shoulder.

She had the door open for him. He got in and yanked the door shut and dropped two boxes of cartridges on the seat between them. He floored the accelerator and the car leaped forward. When he was abreast of the cops he braked hard and she pitched forward, then fell back as he leaned across her and pointed the gun out the window. He squeezed the trigger and the hammer clicked on an empty chamber.

He said, "Shit," and took hold of the wheel again and put the gas pedal on the floor again. He took the corner on two wheels, turned again at the end of the short block.

He said, "Keep an eye out the back window. And hang onto the back of the seat with both hands. I got some fancy driving to do."

She turned obediently and looked out the rear window. She didn't see anyone behind them and told him so.

"They come up in a car? Those two back there."

"No, they were walking."

"That's something. Not that either of

'em's fit to drive, but if they had a car handy they could radio in. The one of them, I didn't hit him but in the arm."

"I know."

"Think I killed the other. Just the thing to make the day complete, isn't it? Nothing takes the heat off a person like killing a cop. Makes other cops know you mean business, and then they know better than to mess with you."

"I thought they really go after somebody who shoots a policeman."

"I was being sarcastic. Still clear in back? Jesus, he had me deader than hell if he knew how to shoot. Wouldn't you think they would teach a cop how to shoot a gun? He had me cold and all he could do was shoot up the rest of the town. Like I said all along."

"What?"

"How things break for you if you stay on top of them. That gas station back in what is it, Grand Island. I had the safety catch on, if you can believe that. Trigger wouldn't move. And then I was forever finding the damn safety and getting it off, and all that time he's just standing there, standing there. He could of picked up anything and come at me and he just stands there, stands there. You know what you just did? You saved my life is what you did."

"I was so frightened. I didn't think I could even move."

"But you did what you had to do. Saved my damn life. I never even thought a cop might be out there waiting for me. Never gave it a thought, just grabbed the shells and figured to be home free. You know what you are?"

"What?"

"Question should be do you know what you *aren't*. What you aren't is a hostage."

"Huh?"

"A hostage. We still had a shot at making it work that way. If they caught us. You could say you were being held prisoner, like we talked about before. Can't do it now, though. You can sit down now. We're far enough out of town so there won't be anything coming up behind us."

She turned around, settled herself in her seat.

"But there's no way you can be a hostage now. Man don't leave a hostage alone in a car with the motor running and expect to find her there when he gets back. And a hostage don't yell to warn him about the police." He shook his head. "That's why I tried to get that second cop. Then the gun comes up empty. Well, that was one time I'd been better off with six bullets in it instead of five. Hell, I should of stopped and reloaded and shot him, but I didn't, and now you ain't a hostage and everybody knows it."

"What does that mean?"

"Means you're an accomplice. Means it'd be a good idea not to get caught. Prison for you, if they catch you."

"What about you?"

"They'd have to kill me to catch me. And I don't feature letting them do that." He threw an arm over the seat back, gave her shoulder a squeeze. "Oh, the hell," he said. "No reason why they should catch either of us."

"HANGING'S too good for them."

FIFTEEN

Between Hondo and Ruidoso a little gravel road wound off to the southeast. He took it for a few miles until he came to an adobe cabin set off by itself. The cabin was a good ways back from the road. There was a small panel truck parked close to the cabin and a beat-up Chevy at the roadside. The Chevy had a key in the ignition. Once he had established that, he got back in the Pontiac and backed it to where it could not be seen from the cabin.

"Now you keep an eye out," he said. "Anybody slows down for a good look, you hit that horn."

He transferred their belongings to the Chevy — their bags, the bag of food, the boxes of shells. The gun, loaded once again, was in place under his belt. He used the Chevy to screen his body from the view of anyone in the cabin, and he covered the open ground rapidly each time he had to move from one car to the other.

From the Pontiac's trunk he took the plates he had removed from the Dodge Coronet before dispatching it over the cliff. He removed the front and back plates from the Chevy and replaced them with the Coronet's plates. When he had finished, he squatted on his heels behind the Chevy's rear fender, his eyes on the cabin. There was no sign he could see to indicate that anyone had observed him.

He returned to the Pontiac. He asked her if she could drive, and she said she couldn't. "You never drove at all?" She shook her head, eyes downcast. "One of these days remind me to teach you," he said. "There's times it comes in handy."

"I'm sorry."

"Oh, don't worry about it."

He went back to the Chevy and started it, certain that the ignition noise must be audible for miles. But no one emerged from the cabin's door or appeared at its windows. He drove it out of sight down the road, then edged back and forth in the narrow road until he had succeeded in turning it back in the direction they had come from. He drove it back past the cabin and parked opposite the Pontiac. He left the engine running and told Betty to get into the Chevy.

Then he parked the Pontiac right where the Chevy had been and ran to the Chevy and drove off grinning.

They were back on the road to Ruidoso before she said anything. He knew she was trying to puzzle it out and he let her work on it.

Finally she said, "What if there was somebody in the cabin?"

"What if there was?"

"Well, isn't he a witness?"

"Sure is."

"But —"

"You didn't want any more shooting, and I thought I'd do what I could to spare your feelings." He had to laugh at the expression on her face. "Oh, it ain't all that complicated. First off, I think there was either nobody home at that cabin or whoever it was was taking a nap. So he's not about to miss that car right away. Fact is, he might take a look out the window and think his car's still there. Pontiac and a Chevy look about the same from a distance. Both of them dark cars.

"But he'll know the difference sooner or later, and that's just fine. He'll call the cops and tell 'em his car's gone and there's another in its place, and they'll get the license plate and know it's the one we were driving, and then they'll know what car we're driving now."

"You're smiling and all, but I don't understand it."

"Well, what are they gonna be looking for? A dark Chevy with New Mexico plates. And we'll be in a dark beat-up Chevy, but that's about as rare as a nigger in a melon patch, and the Chevy we're in has Texas plates on account of that's what I took off the Coronet a million years ago, and I switched the plates."

"I didn't know that. I wondered what you were doing."

"What I was doing is switching plates. They'll be looking for New Mexico plates going to Mexico and we'll be wearing Texas plates and going to Canada."

"Canada?"

"Hell, yes. You got anything against Canada?"

"I don't —"

"Great big country. Cold in the winter, I guess, but that's a ways off in the future. They don't watch the border the way they do in Mexico. Just drive on in and go about your business."

He sped up, overtook a white Volkswagen. He felt a whole lot better now.

Those bennies they sold at the trading post were the best he'd had yet. And they'd been keeping him up just where he wanted to be. The car switch was smooth as you could ask for.

She said something. He didn't catch it and asked her to repeat it.

She said, "How can we get to Canada?"

"Nothing to it."

"I mean it. How can we possibly get to Canada?"

He shot a hard look at her, then softened it right away. "Why, just by driving north," he said. "You just point yourself north and keep pointed that direction for a couple of thousand miles, and you can't hardly help but get to Canada. Big as it is, you'd be hard put to miss it."

North to Albuquerque, west to Gallup. North again through a Navaho reservation. A left turn at Shiprock and across the line into Arizona. A few miles of Arizona and another turn, this time to the right, and they were out of Arizona and into Utah.

Amazing you could be in and out of a state in so little time.

He'd been playing the radio since shortly after they took the Chevy. It wasn't much of a radio, and in the mountains the static was heavy, but he kept it on anyway and listened to it through the static. First there was news of the shootout in Roswell, including the misinformation that the slain policeman had succeeded in wounding his killer in the leg. Later there was a description of the Pontiac. At first the license number was incomplete, but the next time around they had it in full, probably through a records check.

And for awhile that was all they had. Then they found out about the last car switch, and they got it wrong just as he had planned. The license number they were circulating was the number the Chevy had previously borne, not what it now carried. And authorities were certain the car was bound for either Texas or Mexico, and were establishing roadblocks to cut them off. The search was narrowing down now, the announcer concluded, and authorities expected to have the youthful thrill-killer and his teeny-bopper moll in custody before nightfall.

The poor damned fools.

He said, "I never told you about the store. In Roswell."

"What about it?"

"You know, I didn't go in there figuring

on trouble. I walked on in and there's this little round guy behind the counter and a little round woman over at the cash register. I swear they looked like Porky Pig and his girlfriend. What the hell was her name?"

"Pauline."

"Was not. Pauline Pig? Hell."

"Wait a minute. Petunia."

"Petunia. I was about to say Petula like Petula Clark but it was Petunia. Porky behind the counter and Petula, I mean Petunia, over by the register, and a tall skinny guy over by the back wall studying fishing rods. I'd say he looked like Bugs Bunny to make a better story but to be truthful I didn't notice what he looked like.

"So I went up to Porky and put the empty box of shells on the counter and said could I please have two boxes of the same, and he said sure, no trouble, and I thought that was perfectly fine, and then he got out this little old notebook and thumbed it open and asked my name and address. So I made up a name and gave Albuquerque for the address, figuring maybe they couldn't sell to anybody from out of state, and he said he needed the street address, so I made up a number and said Washington Avenue, figuring there might be one in Albuquerque and how was he to know if there wasn't? So he wrote all this down, and Petunia stays at the register and Bugs Bunny puts one fishing pole back and starts getting the feel of another one, and then Porky says he has to see my driver's license."

He shook his head at the memory. "So I didn't see where I had a choice. I tried saying I left it in the car and I was in a hurry but he said it was the law, and I thought the hell with it and pulled out the gun and stuck it in his face. I thought he was about to have a stroke. I said he could give me those shells without any shit or I would blow his fucking head off, and all I can think is the dumb son of a bitch was too rattled to believe me. Or too stupid to think straight. He got all white in the face and kept saying it was the law, he had to see identification to sell me shells, and I told him again what I told him before, and he said again how it was the law, so I just turned and shot his goddamned customer.

"I said, 'Now, damn it, are you goin' to forget the fucking law or do I have to shoot you too?'

"He saw the point then but he just couldn't be cool about it. He brought the wrong shells first time around. I had the sense to read the side of the box even if he didn't and I sent him back for the right ones, and then the damn fool starts telling me the price and trying to figure the tax and reaching for paper to wrap them in, like it still hasn't dawned on him what's happening even with his customer bleeding to death on the floor.

"I grabbed the two boxes. And then I thought how many people I had to kill who never did anything to me, but I just had to kill them so we could get free. And here's this son of a bitch that I really am ticked off at. So I told him he was too damn dumb to live and I shot him, and then I turned and shot Petunia, and then I went outside and there were the cops.

"You know, all I wanted to do was buy those shells. You figure it out."

When they broke into the middle of a record with a bulletin, his hands tightened on the wheel and a pulse throbbed in his temple. It could only be that they knew about the license plates and there was just no way they could know. It wasn't fair. They were home free now and it wasn't fair.

Then he heard the bulletin and the tension left him. The two young thrill-killers had struck again, the announcer chirped. They had robbed a filling station near Van Horn, Texas, just minutes ago and had shot the owner to death and critically wounded one of his employees. Police and Texas Rangers had the area cordoned off with every road blocked, and an arrest was anticipated within the hour.

He glanced at her and laughed at the question in her eyes. "Don't you remember that station? Me and my teen-age moll, we were down in Texas and held up that filling station and shot those two old boys. You mean to tell me it slipped your memory so soon?"

"What happened?"

"Just that we're not the only two people ever shot anybody. Somebody hit that station and they figure it has to be us." He thought for a moment. "Be nice if he got away clean. They'd keep looking down there forever. But I guess we'll hear another version of the story pretty soon."

And they did, but not as a bulletin this time. It was the lead item of the scheduled newscast. The robber had tried to run a roadblock and they gunned him down and killed him. He was a Mexican between thirty and thirty-five years of age driving a pickup truck, and he sure as hell wasn't Jimmie John Hall.

A stop for gas and oil. The kid who filled the tank was trying to grow a mustache and kept touching his upper lip. He never even took a good look at either of them. Jimmie John paid him and they drove off.

Easy as pie now. Just keep going and they got safer with every hour that passed and every mile they covered.

Late in the afternoon he said, "What's the worst thing you ever did?"

"Me?"

"No, the ring-tailed baboon in the rumble seat. Who else would I be talking to?"

"The worst thing I ever did?"

"The thing you're ashamed of the most. From when you were just a little kid."

"The worst thing. I guess — I don't know."

"What were you fixing to say?"

"I don't know. Nothing. The worst thing? I can't think of anything."

"Comes of leading a pure life."

"I mean —"

"You want to know the worst thing I ever did?"

"Okay."

"I can tell you right off. You're thinking it was something since we met. You're wrong. It was, oh, I guess I was eleven or twelve years old at the time. Living with my Ma. We had this house not in the country and not in town. On the edge, you might say. I don't guess you could properly call it a house. What it was, it was a trailer without wheels. She would call it a mobile home, and that's right in there with your plastic glass and green blackboard, because you couldn't pick anything less mobile than a trailer without wheels.

"There was these rats that would come over and eat the garbage. Big old rats. They'd tip the cans over and I'd have to put the garbage back in and hope there wasn't a rat in there waiting to jump out at me. Anyway, I had this slingshot that you sent away for from an ad in the back of a comic book. A Wham-O slingshot. Never forget the name of it.

"Afternoons I would sit out in back of the house, the trailer that is, and I'd be there with my Wham-O slingshot and a pile of pebbles. I'd wait until a rat showed up and then I'd let fly with a pebble. Generally I'd hit one of the trash cans and you wouldn't believe the noise. Never did hit a rat. A slingshot'll have a whole lot of power, but hitting what you aim at is something else again.

"This one day, there wasn't even any rats around, and I don't know how long I was sitting out there in the sun. Anyway, this gray and white alleycat turned up. I used to see him all the time. I don't know if he belonged to anybody. The old woman two doors down would put food out for him. Big tomcat all scarred up from fighting other tomcats.

"So what I did was I took a pebble and shot it at him.

"You know, I never told anybody about this. Course I never told anybody anything before I met you, so that's not saying a whole lot.

"Well, I never expected to hit that cat. I swear I never did. All the times I missed those rats, and by this time I just about took it for granted I would never hit anything, but that pebble hit him just back of the neck and made a sound I'll never get out of my head. I can hear it now just by thinking about it. Long as I live I'll remember it.

"I guess it must of broke his back. He was stretched out there giving out this thin high-pitched whine and moving his front paws like crazy, but his hind paws didn't move at all and I guess they must of been paralyzed. He was shitting and pissing like he had no control of what he was doing. And I knew I had to kill him or die myself of watching him suffer.

"Probably the thing to do was use the slingshot, but I just turned and threw that Wham-O slingshot as far as I could, and I never set eyes on it again. I got the biggest rock I could find and tried hitting him over the head with it. I guess I kept holding back at the last moment, because each time I would hit him and not even knock him out, let alone kill him. And all the while he's making that noise, and I'm smelling his shit and his piss and some other smell I never smelled before and since and I don't know what it was.

"I guess I hit him right after awhile because he died.

"I went out and dug a hole out back and buried him deep as I could.

"And you know what I kept wishing? All the time, over and over, and there's still times when I'll find myself wishing it. That I could find some way to back up the time to that moment when I shot that pebble at him, and this time *not* shoot him. I'll tell you something. I would have dreams where it would happen that way, and I'd wake up and know it was a dream and that cat was dead and no dream would bring him back to life."

"Jimmie John?"

He didn't answer.

"Jimmie John, are you okay?"

"Why?"

"You look funny. You're all sweaty and your face, you just look funny."

He wiped at his forehead. "Just what I was talking about is all. Going back in my mind that way."

"Do you want to stop the car?"

"No. My mind is going too many places at once, that's all it is. I'm all right."

"I'm afraid."

"So am I," he said. "No, I'm not, I just said that. Nothing to be afraid of."

"I can't help it."

He heard the panic in her voice and it touched a nerve. He fought with himself, squeezed tighter on the wheel, bore down more urgently on the gas pedal. His teeth were so tightly clenched that his jaws ached.

"Now it's all right," he made himself say. "It's all right, everything's all right and —"

"What's the matter? Jimmie John?"

"That was a cop car."

"I didn't see it."

"I did. And that mother saw us."

"Are you sure?"

"Stared right at us. Two of 'em and they stared right at us. Turn around, will you? I can't see him in my mirror. You see him?"

"Yes."

"Is he stopping?"

"I think so. Yes!"

"God *damn* it. He's got to turn around. Cost him a little time there." He had the gas pedal on the floor and the Chevy was shimmying slightly. He said, "Damn this piece of shit. Shoulda kept the Toronado. You see him now?"

"No."

"We'll lose him while he turns around. But right now he's calling on ahead and they'll have the road blocked. Oh, damn, do we need another car. Can't stop one, time we stop one he'll be on top of us. Look at this. If I slow down they catch us and if I drive flat out the engine's set to shake itself right out of the car. Clean car and clean plates and no reason to look for us in this part of the country and they have to spot us and I'm damned if I know how."

She was saying something but he couldn't hear her. It was talking about the cat, he decided. That must have been it. It put his mood wrong and threw him out of balance, and when you were out of balance things went wrong as sure as they went right when you were in control. But he had it back together now, he could feel it all coming together, and now all he needed was the littlest good break and they'd be out of this.

He took a corner, tires squealing, and there was his good break.

A car at the roadside. A big long shiny car at the roadside, the other side of the road, pointing the way he would have to go now, pointing back the way they had come from. A big fast car and they would streak right past those cops before they knew what was happening and be fifteen miles gone before they thought to turn around.

He slewed across the road, braked, piled out of the car with the gun in his hand. Big shiny car with a farmer standing up against one fender smoking a cigarette. He ran at the farmer and Betty was getting out of the car and coming after him and he pointed the gun at the farmer and asked for the keys.

The idiot just stood there.

"The keys. You dumb shit, give us those keys!"

"Won't do no good." The words came in a maddeningly slow drawl. "You can't go nowhere in this car."

"You dumb bastard. Do I have to shoot you? You stupid son of a bitch —"

"You can shoot, but you can't drive this car nowhere. Just you look."

He heard a siren approaching. Too late now, even if the idiot gave him the keys. Too late unless —

And then he saw what the farmer was pointing at. The car was up on a jack, its right rear tire off.

"Flat," the farmer was saying. "These roads, and the way they make their tires nowadays."

Two sirens now, one from either direction. Betty just behind him saying, "Oh God, oh God," over and over. The idiot farmer in front of him, talking, talking, and he was flashing the cat and the rabbit and every bad image that ever printed itself on his mind, and there was a band of fire behind his forehead, and he put a bullet through the car's rear window.

"Now that won't help you none," the farmer said.

He shot the left front tire and watched the car settle down a ways before slipping off the jack.

"Well, now," the farmer said.

He shot the dumb son of a bitch.

And turned, the gun in his hand, and the world went into slow motion and his eyes took in everything, registered everything. The police car pulling up on the other side of the road, and another car coming into view from the opposite direction, and Betty with her hand to her throat and her mouth open but nothing coming out, and the cops kneeling down with their car screening them, and the second car braking to a stop on the other side of them, and Betty's hand tightening involuntarily on the Apache tears necklace, and the farmer's blood vivid against the front of his shirt, and the string breaking and little black stones spilling and floating as slowly as feathers to the ground, and —

And Betty screaming.

"Help! He's crazy, he's shooting every-body, he's killing everything!"

Screaming at the top of her lungs and running toward the police.

They always disappointed you. No way you could help that. You expected every-thing and for a time it looked as though they could give everything, for a time, for a time, but in the end it was always the same.

He leveled the gun at her.

They were shooting at him. Bullets whined into the car in back of him, the farmer's car, the car he had already shot to death. But the bullets did not hit him. None of them could hit him.

He drew a bead on her.

And flashed the rabbit, and the tomcat, and the way she looked when she slept.

He turned and threw the gun with all his strength. And turned again. One of the cops was holding her now, letting her sob into the front of his uniform. The other one moved cautiously from behind the car. Other cops from the second car were moving toward him now, their guns drawn, and in the distance he could hear still more sirens.

"Why don't you shoot," he said.

He was still saying it when they reached him.

From: Phil Posmantur
To: Murray Hutter
Subject: <u>HOME</u> treatment (enc.)

Murray --

I'm sending along the treatment for the last act of <u>HOME</u>. Between the novel and some research I've done on the original case, I think I have a good understanding of the dynamics of the principals.

Assuming it's possible to understand them.

I'll let my treatment speak for itself. One minor point, though. Kavanagh describes the gun as a .357 Magnum revolver on a .38 frame, whatever that is. I assume he means a .38 chambered for Magnum loads. Fine. But JJ has trouble with the safety, and as far as I know there's no such animal as a revolver with a safety catch, exc. for very oddball foreign makes. I suppose we either make the gun an automatic or have it jam for some other reason, but could you check with K. and see if I'm off-base on this?

Phil

NOT COMIN' HOME TO YOU
a screen treatment of the last act
BY PHILIP POSMANTUR

We go directly from the capture to the courtroom. Until now we have seen everything through **BETTY** and **JIMMIE JOHN** — one or both of them has been present in every scene, and very nearly every frame, and the only hint of an outside world has come in the impersonal voices heard over the radio. But from the moment of capture their role switches entirely from active to passive. And, just as we see that they no longer have any control over the course of events, we also see that the whole machinery of trial and press coverage has no real relevance, that it is in no way related to who they are.

This is not to say that the story becomes an indictment of judicial procedures or newspapers or even of society itself. But the testimony which we hear, the arguments of attorneys, the conversations of outsiders, the balloting in the jury room, all builds in a brief montage to suggest that neither the two killers nor the rest of society is capable of understanding what exactly did happen, or how, or why.

All of this is handled very impressionistically. There are no full conversations, just fragments of a great many bits of dialogue. Among our fragments are a variety of teen-age bits which hint at the development of Jimmie John as a sort of folk hero for adolescents.

What happens literally is this: They are tried together in Nebraska for the murder of her family, the two defense lawyers more or less cop out on each other, Jimmie John gets the gas chamber and Betty gets life. (In real life, she was a better than even-money bet to get gassed herself, her age and gender notwithstanding. Far as I can determine, she's still inside.)

When sentence is to be pronounced, we end our fragmentary approach. We've just heard the foreman announce the verdict, and we wipe to the sentencing scene, with the judge reading the full sentence to each of them in turn. Through all of this we keep cutting back and forth between the two of them. We see them only in extreme close-up, and we never see the judge.

CUT to a black screen. It's illuminated by the headlights of a car which subsequently drives into frame, and we see that we are in a large parking area where a dozen cars have already gathered. The car takes its place in a row with the others as the camera pulls back to show a high electrified cyclone fence topped with barbed wire which separates the parking lot from the prison grounds. We continue pulling back until we are looking at the scene from THE WARDEN'S POV. He is watching this spectacle through his office window. The car's headlights go out and he turns, shakes his head, and goes back to his desk.

Throughout, we will keep cutting back and forth between the prison interior and the ever-growing gathering of cars outside. Pieces of conversation will establish that these spectators are here for a variety of reasons. There are college types who have come for the same reason they attend anything that can qualify as a Happening — it's all a camp, they're above it, but it's something wacky to do. There are high school boys busy being pseudo-cynical about the whole thing. There are organizer types hung up on technique — going from car to car, getting everybody's lights turned on, everybody's radio turned to the same station, etc. There are adolescent girls who identify strongly with Betty (as well they might; they are distressingly similar to her) and who feel they are making an important gesture. ("I hope they play 'Not Comin' Home to You' at two o'clock. It's his favorite song. It was *their* song." "Do you think he'll hear this inside? He has to hear it, he has to know how we feel.")

What all these spectators feel, what unites them, is a delight in being a part of all this. We gather that there have been many stays of execution and that some of them have been here several times before. If Jimmie John doesn't get wasted tonight, a whole lot of kids are going to feel cheated.

We keep jumping from this mess to Jimmie John's cell, and the contrast of the increasing bedlam outside and the total silence inside is dramatic. He doesn't say anything at all during these glimpses we get of him. When a guard lets him know that tonight is definitely the night, we gather from his nonverbal reaction that he's glad to be getting it over with. They bring him a tray of food. He doesn't eat anything, just ignores it. The chaplain comes. Jimmie John listens stoically for awhile, then just shakes his head and the chaplain stops in midsentence. The prison barber comes to shave him, and we have a close shot of the razor and know that Jimmie John is thinking of taking it away from him, but then he abandons the thought. When the barber goes, he rubs his cheek and shows us that he doesn't think the shave was close enough, but he doesn't care enough to brood about this for long.

The cuts come with increasing frequency as we get closer to the hour set for execution. The cell, the kids outside, the cell, the warden looking at his watch, the cell, the preparation of the gas chamber, the cell, the warden joining some guards and leaving his office, the cell, etc.

When the warden and his party reach the cell, our cuts of the outside feature a disc jockey saying some horseshit to the effect that everybody knows who the next song is being played for, and then, as they open the cell door and collect Jimmie John, every car radio in the lot is playing Waylon Jennings singing "Not Comin' Home to You," and they sound like every car radio in America all playing at once.

They walk down corridors to the gasatorium. When they get there, a really odious **FUNCTIONARY** begins spouting a memorized number on how the best move is to wait until the gas rises and then take the deepest possible breath of it so that you go out as painlessly as possible. The functionary is nervous as hell and Jimmie John keeps giving him the old Muhammad Ali stare, which makes him increasingly nervous. Jimmie John lets him get most of the way through and then suddenly erupts, flinging a guard aside and bellowing. For a second we think he's really going to put up a fight, but the guards have evidently been fully prepared for this contingency. They move right on in and club him to his knees.

From the moment we give Jimmie John a look at the chamber, we quit the intercutting. We just drop the kids cold, Waylon Jennings and all. (I always thought it was Wailin' Jennings, incidentally. Apropos of nothing. . . .)

The functionary resumes his prepared speech, more or less where he dropped it when Jimmie John did his resistance number. He gets all the way to the end, and the same chaplain comes up and says his little piece, and we see that Jimmie

John literally does not hear him. The door to the gas chamber is opened and two guards frogmarch him in and sit him in a chair and strap him in. He gives them no cooperation whatsoever, keeping his body rigid, but they do their job anyway.

We have already heard, in the course of the functionary's prepared speech, an excessively detailed explanation of the manner in which the pellet of cyanide drops into the acid solution, or whatever the hell it does. Now we get to see what we've just heard about. Before the pellet drops Jimmie John fills his lungs with all the fresh air he can hold, to the worried glances of the spectators. The gas rises, and instead of gulping it in as recommended he fights it, holding his breath as long as he possibly can. The gas hits his eyes and they start burning and tearing but he keeps holding his breath until he can't hold it a second longer, and he lets it out and breathes in some gas, but not quite enough to do the job, and he coughs and retches and dies very fucking badly, but dead game all the way.

We cut to the parking area. The song has ended and something else is playing, and when it ends there's a commercial for something, something like Clearasil, and then it ends and there's a tape of six voices in disharmony singing the station's call letters, and another record, and we get the message that the crowd out there does not know the son of a bitch is dead. Two o'clock has come and gone, so he ought to be dead, but they have no way of knowing.

We're in an aerial shot of the sea of cars, and we hold it, and some of the car radios die out, and we hear an engine turn over. A couple of cars drive out of frame and a few more engines start up and we pull back farther and farther, so that we see a good many of the cars moving out and taking different roads away from the prison.

About a third of the cars are still parked, still have their lights on and radios blaring, as we fade very slowly to black.